The Trident of Poseidon

The Trident of Poseidon

donald E carter

Contents

One the mission **1**

Two under the tower **3**

Three Derinkuyu **32**

Four Peru **62**

Five Mt.Nemrut **91**

Six Thermopylae **105**

Seven Home **117**

About the Author **118**

Copyright © 2025 by donald E carter
All rights reserved. No part of this book may be reproduced in any manner whatsoever without written permission except in the case of brief quotations embodied in critical articles and reviews.
First Printing, 2025

{ one }

the mission

We went up to see Chiron only to find a crowd of campers around Chiron and they were staring at us with disgust and we started to push through to find what was wrong.

When he saw us he motioned for us to go inside and then he said to us" someone seemed to have leaked the fact that you are going on another quest."

We looked at one another and then back at chiron and then asked" is that so bad that we get to go on another dangerous mission, I mean we would rather not get killed but the gods chose us.

At that moment we heard the noise outside die down and we went to go check it out and when we went out the door we saw that the camp was returning back to normal and then chiron said with a smile" sometimes all you have to do is ignore them.

Then he said "well there is no time like the present" and he put twenty one more of the magic marbles in a bag and then handed them to us and then he gave us a scroll that had the location that looked like a cricked building and it read: the leaning tower of pisa italy below it.

Chiron got out of the way and we rolled the marbles against the wall and visualized the leaning tower in italy and we stepped through the portal and as we did we started to get drenched because it was raining in italy.

We quickly went for cover and started looking for a glyph that would be a trident on the wall but didn't see one anywhere or on anything and then we went down to the tower base floor and started searching there.

We searched high and low and after a few hours of searching we finally just gave up and I sat down against a wall and fell through and found myself in a hidden room and inside was a statue of poseidon.

I looked it over and saw that the back had a glowing trident on the statue and I called to the others and said" I found it and then the others came through the wall and into the room that it was in.

One by one we touched the glyph and when we did it sucked us in and we started to fall until we hit the ground.

{ two }

under the tower

When we did we got the breath knocked out of us and when we got our breath back we started to look up and noticed that it was as black as the night sky above us.

Then we started to have a look around and soon we had looked around the whole room and then out of the corner of my eye I saw writing starting to appear on the wall.

So I looked at it and saw that it was starting to write the starter note to the first note that will lead to the first clue and I started reading: the first clue will be in the next room next to the royal seat.

Then a door opened and we went up to it and saw a light inside it and we knew that we had to go through that door and when we were on the other side the door collapsed.

We knew that we couldn't go through the way that we came (but why would we). We walked into the room and saw a table with a few chairs but only one had a velvet seat and then while the others were looking at the seat trying to figure out where it was I saw a crown on a wooden seat with a box next to it.

I went up to it and opened the box and saw a small parchment that read :on the far end of the river past the ice and the river of lava and through the rooms with red and green and you'll find the first clue.

We started walking again and soon we found a hallway that seemed to last forever and then finally the hall abruptly ended without warning into a room with emeralds.

We started walking around in the room and then I had to pull the others away into the hallway. Then this hallway seemed to go on for a ways and then it curved to the right.

When it curved to the right we noticed that we were in a room with rubies in it and then one of the rubies, the one that was the biggest began to shine and we started to walk towards it and then I noticed that it was pulling us to it and so I started to push away.

Then I noticed that there were shapes in the crystals surrounding us and I pulled away to the door and on the way grabbed the others and then I pulled them through the door on the opposite side.

When we got away from the crystal we started walking down the hall that we were in and after a few minutes of walking athero said "I'm tired " and then he sat down and he must have pushed a hidden lever or something because a door opened.

We went through the door and I helped athero up and then I went through with him. What was on the other side was an open room with a river of lava that I knew that we couldn't cross.

I took a quick look around and when I couldn't find anything danyelle took a look around and found out that the ground was made of metal and then I noticed the hole in the ground a few feet away.

I started to check out the hole and noticed that a pole could fit in it so I started to look around and almost as soon as I had started looking I found a small part of the pipe and then I started searching again.

After a few minutes of searching I spotted a part of a pipe in the corner of the room and I started towards it and once I got to it I started to pull it out of the ground little by little.

When I got it out of the ground I noticed that it had a grooved end and when I got over to the hole I noticed that the last piece also had a grooved end so I screwed it together.

Then I saw that it wasn't complete and I knew that it had one more piece to find and put together so I started looking again but this one was a little harder to find.

I went all over the room looking all over the place and started looking everywhere and then I finally found it in a barrel in a corner.

When I screwed the last piece in I noticed that there were three keyholes in it and I knew that before we could cross the river of lava we had to find those keys.

We started looking and right off the bat we found the first one of three and I put the first one of the keys into the top keyhole and turned it and a bar came out.

Then after an hour or so of looking I found the second one and I put the second one into the middle keyhole. So we started to look again.

We looked in every corner of every wall and then danyelle fell through a wall and I saw it and then I went after her and when I went through I saw that the third key was hanging from a wall so I grabbed it and went to the lever and put the third key into the bottom keyhole.

When all three keys were in the lever went forward and the gate closed and lava stopped flowing but it wasn't going to hold on for long so we hurried forward towards the opposite bank.

We barely made it to the other side before the lava came again and we started again and once again found ourselves in another hallway and we started to walk down the hall and soon found ourselves in a room filled with ice and I knew what I had to do.

I pulled the others away to the other side of the other side of the room before they could get pulled in by the sight of the crystals.

We went into the next room and it had a regular river in it and we were about to cross when athero said" wait we have to go down the river not across".

We nodded and started back to shore and then we started down the river and soon we had found the chest and we walked up to it and I opened it and inside was a tablet that was gold and It read: cross the river and across the room, don't look down or you will meet your doom. Cross the lava by the blocks beware they sink because they're rocks but before that a puzzle you must break for yours and the world's sake. After you do those go up one stair and down another and skip three doors on the left and go in the fourth.

We up the river again and then I noticed the writings on the wall and I knew that it was the puzzle that I had to figure out and the I pulled athero to the sight and put his brain to the task and as soon as I did he began to move blocks around and soon he had a doorway made in the wall and we walked through and found ourselves in a hidden room.

We walked around and soon we found a lever and when we pulled it we heard a buzzing and then I heard danyelle say" look the river has stopped flowing.

We rushed outside and sure enough the river had stopped flowing and my mind clicked and I motioned for the others to follow me as I crossed it.

Like magic as we were all getting up to the other side the river came crashing down again and we continued on our journey.

We walked down that hallway and then it opened and I knew that if I looked down I'd fall and meet my doom like the tablet said.

Only it didn't mention that I would be balancing on a beam with lava below me and then as I got off I saw the others struggling and one of them almost looked down and when they started to they lost their balance but luckily they were close enough to me that I could catch them.

The others seemed okay at the moment so I turned my back for a second and when I turned back they were holding on for dear life.

I walked across the beam and helped the others across one by one and as soon as I was done doing the last one the beam crumbled and we started walking again.

We took a curve and then another curve and then we were where we were earlier but below and I saw the rocks poking out of the lava and I poked at them. When I did I saw that they were sturdy and I hopped one after another and as I did the others followed.

When we were done jumping from rock to freaking rock and then we turned a corner and soon found ourselves at a three way fork and we chose to go through the left one which led us right back where we started and we came out the center one so we went into the one on the right.

When we came out the other side we saw that we were in a room where there was a hallway to the side otherwise it was an empty room.

We started down the hallway and soon we came to a staircase and we thought of what the verse had said and we started to go up and soon we were at the top and the hallway extended for a few minutes and then we came out in another room and we took a look around and soon I saw a slab of rock that looked like it could be moved.

I motioned for the others to come to me and when they were next to me we pushed the slab with all our might and it moved to reveal a staircase going down.

We started going down the stairs and as soon as we got to the bottom we saw that we were in another hall that had doors mostly on the right but the first thing I noticed was that there were four doors on the left.

So we started counting one …two…three..and when we got to the fourth door we saw that there was just a doorway and in it was a chest that had a scroll in it that read: through this door and to the right and past the crystals that shine so bright.

Go past the woods made of stone in the field made of rock and you shall find the second clue in a hole full of honeydew.

Once I got done reading a door slid open to reveal a passage into a hall so we followed it to find that it began to turn to the left then the right and soon we found ourselves in a room that had a couple of crystals but this couldn't be the one in the scroll because they didn't shine.

So we kept on going out the door to the left and after a while we found a room with sapphires and rubies but they didn't shine like the scroll said so we left that room as well.

Then we saw a light in the distance that we hoped was the crystals but when we got there we saw that it was only a torch and we saw that it was also one that was one of ours.

We walked back the way we had come and noticed that there was another door that was half hidden in shadow and I motioned for the others to follow me.

We went down that hallway and soon we had found the crystals that had been mentioned in the scroll and after a few moments of looking at them I had to pull away because I could feel myself being pulled in.

So I snapped out of the trance and noticed that the others were in the same trace so I went over to them and pulled them out of the room and soon they were themselves again.

We started walking again and after about an hour I began to see light again and I saw that it was coming from above so we started to peel back rock little by little and soon we came into a room that was a heck of a lot brighter than where we were.

We saw that the room had a door and I could see light on the other side and so we looked closer and saw that the door wasn't really a door, it was a giant rock in front of the hole.

So I motioned for the others to push with me and together we moved the giant boulder that was in front of the hole.

We went through the hole into the bright room beyond but we still were not in the big field made out of rock.

So we went through the door to the left and we were back in another hallway. We walked down this hallway and started to open doors but none of them was the way to the field so I just kept walking.

Then all of a sudden we stepped out in the open and I saw that we had found it...the field was at our feet.

We walked across the field but there weren't any trees in sight then I remembered what it said about stone trees but still didn't see any.

Then I saw the giant door with the locks on it and I knew what we had to do so I walked up to it and we looked at each other and started looking for the three keys.

After a few minutes I saw something small sticking out of the ground and so I went up to it and pulled on it and barely got it out and saw that it was the first out of three keys that we had to get.

I went up to the first lock and put the key into the keyhole and turned it and it clicked open. So the hunt for the second key began and it took about an hour to find and I wasn't even the one to find it.

I turned around as I heard a click and saw that Danyelle was walking away from the locks and the second one was unlocked so I started looking for the third and final one and it didn't take long to find because it was already in there.

I reached up to where the last lock was and turned the key and the door swung open to reveal the other side of the field and we went through as it was opening and we saw the rock trees in the distance.

We started walking again and soon we had reached the trees made of rock and we started through them and that is when we saw the hole in the wall in the distance in front of us.

After about an hour of walking we arrived at the chest but we stopped to admire the plant growth and then I opened it and inside was another golden tablet.

I reached into the chest and pulled out the tablet and it read: go through this door and down the way through the corridor and out the bay past the rubies, sapphires, and emeralds too and you find the third note to the third clue.

As I was finished reading the back of the hole slid open revealing a space behind it and we went through the hole and immediately we were dropping again.

When we landed we landed in water and we got all soaked. When we had gathered our wits we started swimming towards land and soon found it and as we got onto land I noticed the hallway to the left and I started towards it.

We walked down the tunnel and soon we were in a quartz crystal room and I knew that there was no writing on it in the tablet and so we continued walking.

We continued down the passage and soon we were in another room and this one had only rubies but nothing else so we continued walking and soon we came into another room but the door out of the room was locked and as we passed through the door we just came through it shut behind us and I knew that we were trapped.

We saw that there was a puzzle and I put athero up to the task and as usual he went right through it in speeding colors.

As he was putting the last piece in place the exit door opened to reveal the passage but I saw that the passage was full of sand and stones so I knew that there had to be quicksand on the ground so I said to the others "watch out there is quicksand ,stay on the rocks".

I jumped from one rock to the next and soon I was across and I motioned for the others to do the same thing as I had done.

As soon as we were all across we started down the hall again and almost right after we had got away from the quicksand we found our way to a room with sapphires in it but the other stones were missing so we just kept walking again.

We continued to walk down the hallway and soon we were in a room with emeralds in it but again the other stones were missing so we went through the door to the left and continued down the hall.

We went around a bend and I saw sparkles on the wall of red , blue, and green and I knew that we were close to the room that we needed to be in .

At that moment we walked into the blazing light of the crystals and soon the others were hooked onto the crystals and I knew that if I didn't get out of there soon with the others then we would all be hooked.

So I grabbed the others and I saw three switches one for each gem and then I knew that we all had to grab one but first I had to get back in the right place.

So I pulled the other two into the last room we were in and began to shake them and as they came to they began to shake their heads as if clearing their heads from a dream.

Once I got everyone back on board we went back into the other room and I showed them the switches and they each went to one of them.

Danyelle went to the ruby one and athero went to the sapphire one and that left me with the emerald one.

At the same time we pulled the levers and as we did a hidden door opened up revealing a secret passage. We climbed through the hole which was the door in the wall and started to walk down the hallway that was behind it .

We continued as the passage got smaller until we could barely fit and then we came out in a room that had to be made for smaller people because we had to stoop and we went out of the room and into a larger hallway and soon we were standing in front of an alter and I saw that it had skid marks on the bottom and I began pushing it to the side.

As soon as I got it pushed over to the side I saw that it had a set of stairs leading down and so as I started down I waved my hand to the other two to follow and we went down the stairs together.

When we got to the bottom we noticed that to the right there was a tunnel leading off and to the left there was a small chest and so we went over to the chest and opened it and inside was the third note to the third clue.

I picked it up and it said: go down the hall and to the left past the skeletons and pass the riddle and go through the arched doorway and pass the crystal poles and pipe the colors on the poles and you shall open the next room and the next clue is hidden inside.

We started walking for a few minutes and went to the tunnel to the left and continued to walk down the hall and then we came to a wall but as we watched there began to be symbols etched into the wall.

I reached out to touch it and it sucked me through into a room that we didn't know about and we started to have a look around and soon we saw a small space but it was too small for any of us to go through.

So we started looking again and after looking for another minute we found another hole that was a little bigger but we still couldn't fit so we continued looking and then I noticed the skeletons and I walked up to them and saw that they were guarding a door that was closed.

I started looking the door over and noticed that the door was locked so we started looking for a key and then I saw something shiny in the corner of the room and so I went to it and saw that it wasn't the key but it looked like it opened something so we started looking around and soon I saw a small jewelry box that seemed out of place and so I went up to it and put the metal into it and pressed it in and it clicked and swung open.

As it opened it squeaked and I knew that it had to have been here awhile and inside was a bunch of pictures and then something metal dropped and I looked down and saw that it was the key.

I picked it up and went to the door with it and pushed it in and turned the key clockwise and I could hear clicking as I was doing so and then the door swung open suddenly and I barely got my hands out of the way.

We went through the door and soon we were in another part of the same hallway and we kept following it and started to see skeletons laying here and there and in one corner I saw a pair of skeletons under a rock and then I looked around I saw that we were in a room with a bunch of skeletons and I began to wonder if we would be next.

Then I noticed that the skeletons all had one thing in common. They all were in awkward positions like they were put there on purpose and I saw the door on the opposite side begin to close and I knew what would happen next.

So we looked at one another and rushed past that door and the last thing I saw was the spikes coming out of the ceiling and we turned around and began to walk again and then we took a right and we saw a mummy up ahead and as we approached it seemed to come alive.

When we got within ten feet of it it began to speak in a raspy voice and said" what do you call a dumb bug".

We thought for a moment and after quick thinking we almost spoke out of turn but we went back to each other and then we came to a conclusion and we stood up straight and said together "a spider" and to our astonishment the mummy swung forward and we walked out onto a field that had three poles in it in a triangle and a triangle in the middle of the field.

So we walked ourselves to the triangle and I saw a pipe on the edge

Of the triangle and I knew what I had to do and put the pipes to my lips and blue on the one with the color red and then the color blue and lastly the color green and then they all lit up and then a rumbling started and a door at the far end of the field opened up to reveal a new passageway.

When we saw what had happened we started walking up towards the door and when we got there we saw that there was a chest in the center of it but it was locked but there wasn't any keyhole in sight so we started looking over the chest and then I discovered something weird.

It had buttons on the bottom of it and so I held the chest up while athero pushed all sorts of buttons on the bottom and then I heard a click and I quickly turned it back over to its right side up and we opened it to look inside.

When I opened the chest there was a bright light emulating from it and as the light faded I noticed that there was another tablet inside so I picked it up and started to read it.

It said: go down the hall and through this door and pay the rich to feed the poor and pass the crystals in red then blue never fret because you are not thought to find the crystals with the tinted hue and you'll find what is overdue.

At that moment as we were finished reading a door opened to the right of us and we started forward and almost immediately I had to pull athero back because he almost got swallowed up by sand and then I saw that there was quicksand everywhere and I knew that we had to be careful.

Then I saw the holes in the wall and I got an idea so I started climbing across the wall putting my shoes in the bottom holes and holding onto the top ones with my hands.

When the others saw what I was doing they began to do the same thing and pretty soon we were all acoss and on our way.

I slowly put my foot down and then I saw that it was solid ground and I motioned for them to follow me and I started walking down the hall with them on my heels.

Then we came to a fork and we saw lights in two of them and I knew that there had to be a turn around and we agreed to take the one on the left where there were no lights and soon we found out why.

When we got to the next room we saw that there was a chest in the corner and we had thought that we had found a shortcut but I knew that something was wrong with this picture.

I hurried them out of the room in a rush and the next thing I knew the walls slammed shut and if we would have been there we would be squashed like a pancake in a waffle maker.

They wiped their foreheads and thanked me and then we started moving again and soon we came out into a big room and we saw that it was filled with rubies all over the ceiling and the walls.

Then I noticed myself being dragged and I put my feet down and pushed against it and it stopped and I knew that we had to get out of that room and into the hall again and as we were getting into the hall I started thinking to myself "I miss the old days".

We started walking down the hall and soon we saw the brilliance of some sapphires bouncing off the walls of the cave and soon we turned into a room that was filled to the brim with sapphires and they were everywhere.

On the ceiling, walls and also sprouting up from the ground and I knew that we couldn't stand to stay in this room for long.

Soi pushed the others to the doorway on the other side and as I was doing this the crystals began to blink and then flash and then the buzzing started and before we knew it the room exploded and rocks rained down from the ceiling.

We turned to go through the door just in time and when we did we couldn't go back.

So we started walking again and we started to see that we were where we could see through the dust.

Then I noticed the hallway leading off to the right and I grabbed athero who in turn grabbed danyelle and we went through that hallway door and into another room that was filled with amethyst this time.

But the amethyst that was growing here was faintly glowing as if it was a mass of something inside of it and I started to walk towards it without thinking and I was almost to it when I caught myself.

Then when I caught myself I started to back up but it was like it was calling me....calling my name and I just couldn't ignore it no matter what I tried and I knew that I couldn't keep away from it so I motioned for the other two and they knew what had to be done.

They grabbed me by the arms and started to drag me out of the room and then as they did the voices stopped and I was able to regain control.

Then as I was looking over my body I noticed the chest in a corner of the room that we were just in and I said "go to the chest and bring me that paper".

They rushed over to the chest and apparently it wasn't locked and they brought the paper back to me and reread it in all of our heads.

It read: go down the hall and past the secret room, follow the buzz in the air, don't cheat down the board so play fair and you will get the next clue.

We dropped the paper and started walking down the hall and soon the wall ended and I touched it but I wasn't sucked through like last time.

So we started wandering the hall and then as usual athero sat down by the wall and a door opened and we pulled athero back and we went through the door.

When we came though the other side of the door we saw that we were in the secret room that it mentioned but there didn't seem to be any exit now that the door had closed behind us.

We started looking for a door or something like one and after a while of not finding one we decided to look one more place and that was behind where a bed would be and when we got the box that was in its place scooted out of the way we saw that there was a hole there.

We tried to fit through it but it was much too small for us and so we started looking again and soon we found a much bigger hole behind the cabinet.

We went through that hole and saw that we were near the chest because the tablet that I had kept at the beginning of our journey started to vibrate and we just started moving with the buzz and then we must have walked too far away because it stopped.

So we started to go the opposite direction and saw that it was buzzing again and I knew that it would lead us to the next chest.

We continued to follow the buzzing and after a few minutes It started to grow faint so I turned until it grew and then I started walking again.

After a few minutes of walking it led me into a dead end and then I got mad and punched the wall and electricity came out and the wall collapsed.

Showing us a room that was hidden and then we knew that this was the hidden room and the vibrating was getting really strong right around this area and we started to search for the chest but couldn't find it so I used the tablet to find it and then as the vibrations were getting too hard I saw the chest but it looked different from the others.

we walked up to it anyway and went to open it and soon we were almost blinded because this one was the brightest one yet and when the shine wore off I picked up the tablet and read it.

Go down this hall and past the never ending river through the veil of enchantment and past the river of the red water and you shall find the next note.

We saw that there was a doorway that opened up nearby and when we went to it we saw that there was a hallway in front of us.

We looked at each other and then started down the hall. After a few moments we came to a room that didn't seem to have another way out so we started looking around to try to find the way out.

Then athero noticed the hole behind the chair in the corner and we went to it and started to move the chair and then we went into the hole and on the other side was a raging river in an enormous room and I knew what we had to do.

So we started searching for a pipe that would go in the hole by the river and after a few minutes athero found the first part of the pipe(apparently there were three pieces).

Then I put that piece into the hole but it was obviously the wrong piece so we continued looking and then I found the second piece and when I put it with the first piece it melded with the first and started to look like a lever but we were still missing the bottom.

So we went back to looking again and once again athero found the bottom but instead of giving it to me he stuck it in and I saw him do it so I went over to him and put the other two into the hole with the bottom and then it slid in and we pulled it and a blockage came up blocking the river.

When that happened we hurried across because it didn't look like it would hold for long and as we were reaching the other side the blockage broke and the water came pouring down and we jumped onto the other shore so the water wouldn't get us.

When we got to the far shore we started walking again and soon we came upon an archway that was standing by itself but was connected by two walls.

We looked closer and we saw that it had a veil in it and so we decided to try to go another way but when we reached the far side of the rock it wouldn't let us go any further so we went back and we knew that we would have to go through the veil and we didn't know where it would lead or if it would kill us even.

We walked forward and before I knew it I was getting pushed out of the other side.

When I got pushed out I took a look around and then I saw the others coming out of the veil and together we stepped forward and then we noticed the river of lava and I also noticed the transport pad.

I stepped onto the transport pad and then I had athero pull the lever that was right beside the lava and the pad went over the lava to the other side and then I saw a switch on my side and I pull it and the pad went back and the last two stepped onto the pad and it barely transported the other two at the same time over the river of lava.

We started to have a look around and soon we saw a chest in the corner by a stone window and we walked up to it and I opened the chest and inside was a note that read: go through the wall and into the corridor down the hall into the field unlock the door that needs unlocked and you shall find the next clue.

We saw a shiver go across part of the wall and I knew that it was the part of the wall that we had to walk through and we started to walk forward but when we did I noticed that there were tiny trees in front of it.

Danyelle and athero walked forward and automatically the trees started to grab their ankles and I knew that we had to hop through the wall.

So I pulled them back and the trees returned back to normal and I showed them what had to be done and I hopped over the trees and through the wall and the others saw what I did and soon they followed.

When we got through the wall we noticed that we were in another hallway and then we started walking again and soon the wall turned from red to stone brown and the hallway got thinner and shorter and I knew that we had to be in the corridor.

We continued down the corridor for a few minutes and it seemed to last forever and then it skimmed down so much that we had to get down on our knees.

Then it opened up into a large room and I knew that we had to get out of that room as soon as possible because I had a feeling of dread in my body from the moment that we got into the room and then I saw it, two glowing eyes.

I pushed the others toward the door on the far end of the room and out of the corner of my eye I saw a shadow emerging and we ran through the door and slammed it shut and then we locked it from the side that we were on.

We started walking again and soon we found the field and when we got to the field we stopped and started to glance around but there wasn't any door in sight so we started walking again and soon we broke through another veil and when we did we saw the door and we started to go towards it.

When we got to the wall where the door was, we saw that it was protected by a shield and I quickly knew how to break it.

I took a long pipe and banged it against the shield until it turned red and then it shattered and we walked forward and then we saw that we had to find four keys.

We started looking around for the first key and soon we found it and I put it in the first keyhole and it automatically turned and then we set out to search for the second key and after a hour of searching athero finally found the second key and he came up to me all smug and handed it over smiling the whole time.

I looked at him and then I turned around and put the second key into the keyhole and it also turned and we started looking for the third one and soon found that one almost right off the bat.

I brought it to the door and put it to the third keyhole and as the others did, it turned as well. So we started looking for the final one and then I noticed that the door was open and I saw that the final key was already there.

We started walking into the room beyond the door and soon I had spotted the chest and I went over to open it and I had to cover my eyes so it didn't blind me and then it shimmered down and I was able to pick up the tablet and we gathered around and read the tablet.

It read: go past the garnet and through the veil past the rivers that are twins but weak so don't be afraid to get wet and the note to the next clue you will get.

We started walking again and soon we started to come by some doors and we opened them one by one and the last one just had a rock wall behind it.

So we started walking again and soon we walked into a room that had a ton of emeralds in it and we knew that we had to find garnet and so we just passed through that room and soon found ourselves in a room with rubies and we just passed right through that room as well.

The next room however was filled to the brim with garnet and they were shining like crazy. Then I noticed the door at the far wall and I began to push the others through it.

When we got through the door we started forward again and we started looking for another veil like the one we went through before.

After a few minutes of looking we came across an empty one and we knew that this wasn't the right one so we started looking again.

We looked everywhere that we thought it would be and then we came back to the veil that was empty before but it now had a shimmering and so I walked into it and I was soon spit out on the other side.

After a few moments the others came through and toppled over each other and then they stood up and brushed themselves off and we started walking again.

After a few minutes we came to a river and I knew that it had to be the first of the twin rivers and I started to cross and as I did the current started to get stronger as if the water was getting stronger and I just kept going until I was on the other side.

Then I motioned for the others to follow and I said "it's not as bad as it looks." They nodded and started across and soon they were next to me all wet and we started walking again.

Then after a few minutes we came to the other river of the twin rivers and we began to cross this one as well but this one was a little rougher so we had a little bit of trouble getting across this one but we finally got there and when we got to the other side we started to look around and soon we found a chest that looked like the one that would hold the note and so we opened it and it was empty.

We kept searching and after a good five minutes we finally found another chest that looked almost identical to the first and we opened it to find the paper inside so I picked it up and I read it.

The paper said: go across the plain and unlock the door and inside you will find one more go through that one and down that hall and you will find the clue to the seventh call.

We started walking and after a few minutes we saw light in the distance but it didn't seem like natural light and as we got closer we noticed that it was the plain that it was talking about and soon we were walking across the plain and then we saw a sight that said: don't drink the water.

We walked past that sign because we didn't intend to drink the water and soon we were at the door and it had four locks on it and this time there were no keys in the locks and we had to find all of them.

We started looking for the first key and after about an hour or two we finally found the first key and it was athero who found it (I swear that kid is like a magnet).

I brought the key to the first lock and put it into it and it turned like the last time and then we started looking for the second key and soon he had found another one(I swear)but instead of giving it to me I let him put it in and it turned just the same.

Then we started looking for the third one and to my surprise it was danyelle who found it this time and she brought it to me and as she did our eyes met and I put the key into the door and then we started looking for the fourth and final one.

We started searching high and low until we couldn't search anymore and then we all sat down but as danyelle sat down she sprung back up(like a spring chicken) and when she looked down she saw that she had sat on the fourth key and it was sticking out of the ground all rusty.

Then she brought the key to the last lock and it came off and the doors opened and we walked into the room beyond.

When we walked into the room we noticed that there was another locked door but this one only had one lock and we started searching for the key to this door and then I noticed the size of the key.

It was huge and then I saw it in the corner and I began to drag the key over to the lock and the others saw what I was doing and began to help and once we got it to the lock we put it in and pushed it into the lock and turned and it opened.

And it opened into a hallway and it wasn't just any hallway it was a hidden hallway and so we went through that door and started to go down that hallway and we began to hear vibration and I opened my bag and took out the tablet and it was glowing again faintly and also vibrating and I noticed the last time I did this it led me to the clue so I followed the tablets light and soon we were in a room that was filled with jewels and in the corner was a chest that I followed the light of the tablet that I was holding to.

When I got to the chest I put the tablet in my hands back into my bag and opened the chest and I knew that I had to cover my face and when I did the bright light went away quite quickly.

When it went away I read it and it read: to the left and down that hall drop down and embrace the fall in the pond you must go through the bottom and out the top and on four letters you'll have to hop, the big three will help along the way but that is all I have to say.

We looked around and saw a hallway going off the left part of the room and so we went into it and as we were walking down that tunnel I began to think on how the three brothers were going to help us in this quest.

I was so lost in thought that I didn't see the hole and I sort of fell through it and landed in water that was at the bottom of the hole and then I saw the others drop in and I said" have a nice fall".

Then I saw that they dove down to the bottom and I put my head underwater to see where they were going and I saw a hole at the bottom and I resurfaced and then dove again towards the hole and I followed them through it and the underwater tunnel was so long that I almost burst.

When I went out of the water my lungs nearly burst and I gulped in as much air as needed and then I started swimming towards the shore.

When I got to the shore I laid on my back for a second and tried to catch my breath. When I had caught my breath I started to look around and the first thing I noticed was a door going off to the right.

I went through the door and found the others in the next room and they turned and looked at me and said" we were wondering when you were going to show up."

I returned that with a sly grin and we started looking for a way out and I was about to reach for a lever when my foot started to go down.

When I felt that I could feel a feeling of dread and I thought that it was a trap and so I ducked as did the others and then a door opened that was mirroring part of a wall.

We went through rather fast because as soon as I took my foot off the stone the door began to close. So I ran for the door and barely made it through it to the other side.

What I found on the other side was a large room full of letters so I took a look around and saw a question that needed to be answered and the question was simple: who is your father?

I had played plenty of video games to know what I had to do and that is to step on the letters that would spell out my fathers, name.

I walked over to the "z" and started to spell zeus and I noticed that as I spelled it out it spelled it on the paper and after a few minutes I had it spelled and then I heard a loud "ding".

Then we fell through the floor and under the floor was another room but this one was not as big but it did have a chest in the corner and in front of the chest was a fake window that could possibly be a hidden door.

We went up to the chest and opened it and inside was a note that read: through the door in front of you is the one that you must go through to find the lever to open it and then go down the hall and to the left and cross the chasm and you shall find the next clue.

We stared at it for a few minutes then I started looking around and soon I saw something sticking out of the wall so I went over to it and I saw that it was a lever and then I knew what I had to do.

I pulled the lever and then I heard a rumbling and the back of the fake window slid open into a door that we could go through.

'when I got a good look inside I saw that it had opened into a hallway.

We were weary of going into this hallway though because it was full of spider webs and we could hear scuttling inside and we knew that there had to be giant spiders inside.

We finally took up the courage to step into the hallway and then the door shut behind us and we could hear them coming for us.

Then I saw the eyes in the distance and then I put myself in the lead and we went toward the spiders and as they tried to attack us I shot off one lightning bolt after another and after a few moments of doing this the spiders got aggravated and started to attack more aggressively and I was throwing lighting every which way and then they all disappeared and then we found out why.

Out of the darkness came a giant looming shape that was in the shape of a spider but this shape was twenty times the size of the biggest spider that we had fought before.

Without thinking as soon as I saw the eye of this thing I shot a huge lightning bolt at its eye and nailed it right on the spot.

It swayed and while it did I stood motionless and then we saw that it had disappeared and then we walked closer and soon we were on the edge of the cliff and in front of us was the chasm that was in the note.

I started looking around with what little visuals I had and saw that there was a line of vines near the ceiling of the cave but we still needed to find a way to get to them.

So we started to climb because when I was looking around I saw a ledge that might reach the first vine. After a few minutes I made it to the first part of the ledge and I started crawling across it with the others behind me and after a few minutes we got to the end of the ledge.

When we got to the edge I reached out for the vine and got a hold of the first one in line and I started to climb onto it and to my surprise it didn't fall and I started to swing until I could grasp the second one.

Then I got onto the second one and then as I swung from one to the next one the rest followed until we reached the other side.

Once we reached the other side we went towards the far wall and I saw the chest in the corner and so I went up to it and opened it.

When I did I had to cover my eyes again and as I did the glare quickly faded and I picked up the tablet and when the others came up to me they looked over my shoulder and we read it.

This is what it said: go through the door to the left and down the hall past the arch and past the ark and through the river and down the slope and you'll find the next note.

As we were reading we didn't notice the door forming out of the wall to the left of us and then when we got done reading we looked around and saw the door after a few minutes.

We went through the door and it stretched out into a hallway and we started down that hallway and it seemed to take forever.

As we were walking we saw several things and then something caught my eye and then I realized why. The thing that I was staring at was an arch.

I turned and started walking towards it and when I got to it I saw a door in the far wall and I started towards it and then as I reached it I motioned for the others to follow me and I went through it.

When we went through the other side we started forward and we started moving again and soon we were in another hallway and it was darkening so before it got too dark I grabbed a torch and I lit it.

Then we continued walking and soon all around us was pitch black and then it started to get light again as we reached the edge of the tunnel.

Then the tunnel ended and opened up into a room where in the center was a small wooden toy ark that was almost identical to Noah's ark.

We walked around the room because it didn't seem to have an exit but we knew otherwise so we started checking walls and moving things and soon we found a hole in the wall where one at a time could fit and we went through it.

When we went through to the other side we saw that on the other side was a river and there was a lever on the other side so I knew what I had to do.

So I started to cross the river but the farther I got the harder it got until it was almost carrying me away and I was almost across and then I got to the other side of the river.

Then I went to the lever and pulled it and the river started to slow down and the others were able to cross now.

Once we were all on the other side we headed to the next room and I started down the hill that was on the other side of the river and then I saw the chest that was near a wall along with some boxes.

So we opened the chest and covered our eyes but there was no tablet so we started to destroy boxes and then I saw a light coming from the wall and I started to peel off part of the wall.

Then to our surprise there was a note instead we covered our eyes until we realized that there was no table.

We were disappointed that the tablet wasn't going to be there and we looked at it and I waited until the others were ready and then I read it in my head and it read: go through the vines and into the hidden hallway, down the hill and up the stairs go through the door with two keys needed and through the lake that is weeded and you will find the next clue.

At that moment a door opened and we went through and we knew that it would close behind us but it didn't just close it shuttered the hallway when it rolled across.

However there was still light inside the tunnel that we were in and at the end of the tunnel I could see that it abruptly ended.

We walked up to the end of the tunnel and then I saw the vines and I motioned for the others to follow me. I moved the vines and there was a wall but there were markings on the wall.

So I started to feel over it and then I saw the hole and the lump and I pushed the lump over to the hole and the door swung aside revealing a secret hallway.

We went through rather quickly thinking that it would roll back any moment and we wouldn't be able to get through again.

Once we were through the door closed and we were locked in the dark but our eyes adjusted rather quickly and we saw that we were in a hallway that led to a slope that led down and so down we went.

Once we were down the slope the hallway began to curve and we saw a staircase up ahead and we knew that we had to climb it although it was a stair that looked like it went up forever and then as we started up the stairs we decided not to look down.

We were climbing for about an hour and then we came out at the top and then athero looked down and almost fell back to the bottom but I steered him back towards us and then after he got his sickness taken care of we started again.

We kept walking and then we came into another field and at the end was another door but there were only two keys that needed to be found for this door.

So we started searching for the first key and after about an hour of searching athero yelled something in old greek and then he came running up to me holding the first key and so I put it in the first hole but it didn't fit so I tried the second one and that one it did.

Then we started searching for the first key since we already had the second one and after a few minutes danyelle found the other one and brought it to me.

I went up to the other lock and put it into the first one and the door opened to reveal a swampy room that half the room was covered in swamp and the other half was made of brick.

We started to wade through the swamp and soon we started to see bubbles and we knew that there was something in the water and so we hurried across and almost all of us were on the brick side when it emerged.

What had emerged was a shadow and it was in the shape of a worm. Then it shimmered and disappeared and athero walked up to us and we walked up to the chest and opened it and had to cover our eyes because unlike the last time there was a large shimmer where the tablet was and after the shimmer cleared I picked up the tablet and wiped it off because it was dusty and then I read it.

It read:if you don't want to reach your doom then purify the swamp to get to the next room first find the help that you'll need in the form of a potion and this will grant you spirit motion, then find the help of a fairy and this will make the swamp nice and airy.

We went through a door to the left and on the side table was a couple of bottles and in one of the bottles was a liquid and I picked it up and it said" fairy powder" and we looked at one another and we went into the swamp but we were just getting wet.

Then we knew that we had to find something else and we started looking for another door but there didn't seem to be one in sight.

At that moment I noticed a seal behind one of the paintings on the wall and so I walked out of the swamp and over to the painting and pulled it off the wall and I saw that there was a large hole in the wall but there wasn't inside so we put the picture back on the wall.

Then I noticed the lever sticking out of the water and I went over to it and pushed it over. When I did there was a buzzing sound and a clink and then I started towards the picture again but when I was nearly there I stubbed my foot on something.

So I put my hand into the water and I felt another lever and so I pushed that one down and then I heard another buzzing and another click and when I reached the picture there was still nothing in it but the bottom was half way open.

Then I knew that I had to find two more levers and that would open the bottom all the way and then I started to search the swamp and almost right away I found the third lever but I had to really search for the fourth one.

Once I had those two flipped over I went back to the picture and sure enough there was a bottle in it and I picked it up and I read it and it said chakra weaver.

On the front of it was a label that read: don't drink unless needed.

I looked at it and saw that there was just enough for the three of us to have a sip.

I took the fairy powder out of my pocket and put it into the water and then once I had done that I pulled out the bottle that I had just got and took a sip and then I stepped into the swamp and then I was sinking rather fast and then I was in another room.

I waited for the others and an hour went by and then two and then finally the others came through and then I figured out why it took them so long.

I had the fairy powder and the other bottle and they had to do it the hard way.

When we were all finally down there we saw that we were in front of a chest and the chest was on the table.

When we walked up to it we saw that it was chained to the table and on the chest was the note that said: to save the world you must endanger it first.

We opened the chest and smoke poured out and we knew that it was a spirit and we would have to defeat whatever it belonged to soon.

We looked at the tablet and saw that it read: down the hall and to the right buckle up you're in for a fight behind the worm is the piece you seek and from its wrath that you will have to release.

We looked around and didn't see any doors on the first look around but on the next one there was a door in the middle of the wall (I don't know how I missed that).

We went through the door and soon we were in another hallway but not long after we got into the hall curved to the right and we had no choice but to follow it .

Then out of nowhere the tunnel ended into a room and in front of us was a chest and we were confused as heck because we thought we would be getting the trident piece.

We started walking up to the chest and was about to it when the shadow reappeared but this time it didn't fade away instead it solidified.

Once it was done solidifying it attacked and danyelle tried to go for the box but was smacked with its tail and went flying into a wall.

I rushed over to her but I ended up getting hit as well and then I saw that she was okay and we began to fight it because that seemed to be the only way we was going to beat it and so I started throwing lightning bolts and every time I did it shuttered and after a few minutes of doing that it started to go through the floor.

Once we had got it a few hundred more times it was almost through the floor and then it disappeared and we reached the box.

We walked up to it and opened the box and inside was the bottom of the trident and I picked it up and I could feel the power in it.

We all knew what we had to do next and we all picked out a marble and rolled it against a wall and thought of Derinkuru turkey.

Then we stepped through the portal to our destination and soon we were in a different landscape and in front of us was the broken down city of Derinkuru.

{ three }

Derinkuyu

We started walking around the city and then we noticed a hole in the ground and I turned to the others and they both agreed that we had to go down that hole (at least to see it the glyph was down there).

We started down the hole and then the ladder stopped but the hole didn't and then all of a sudden the ladder broke and we fell to the bottom of the hole which wasn't very far but it was dark and then we began to see a light and I walked up to it and I saw that it was a green trident and I yelled at the others "I found it".

They rushed over and we reached out and touched it at the same time and then we were falling for what seemed like forever but we had landed on water but it seemed like we were still falling.

When I figured out that I wasn't falling anymore I got to my feet and started walking around to try to find the other two and found them not too far away.

When we had gathered again we knew that we would find the clue to the first note in the next room and we started walking to the next room and soon found it.

When we got to the next room we saw that it was a room with crystals and there were lights in them. Danyelle picked one of the crystals and shined the light on the wall and then the words started to become visible to the human eye.

As it became visible we began to read it and it said: go towards the entrance and go to the dark and you'll find an undying heart, put it in the water and watch it gleam and the wall will show a glowing seam.

We started back to the entrance where we had fallen in and saw a place of dark near the wall and we started searching the dark for a heart of some kind and then I knocked my head.

I looked up and saw an empty torch and I reached into my bag and pulled out some matches and after the third one I got it lit.

I put it to the ground and started looking again and then I saw a glitter and I knew exactly what kind of heart it was now.

Near me was a small crystal clear heart necklace and I picked it up and put it into the water and soon we saw a rip in the wall and we started to see it and when we got there we saw that it was a door that we didn't notice before.

I pulled at the wall and then when the other two saw that I needed help opening the door they began to help pull at the door as well and together we opened the door and on the other side was a room that was like a bedroom.

We walked into it and soon a chest caught my eye and I knew that the first note was going to be in there so we walked over to the chest and opened it and inside was a paper that said: go through the door in front of you pass by this note and into the next room and through the traps that I had laid out for you cross the lava and open the one lock door and inside you will find the first clue of many which reside.

At that moment a door slid open in front of us. We started walking and went through that door in front of us.

When we went through the door we found ourselves in a hallway and as we walked down the hallway we noticed the color of the walls changing.

Then we came into a room that was a lot different than the last one.

We started walking and then I tripped and the others almost got their heads chopped off and I noticed that the reason I tripped was because of a trip wire.

We quickly passed that one and then after a few moments danyelle stepped on a stone and we had to duck and after a few moments we got up again and she ended up stepping on the exact same stone and we had to duck again.

She almost stepped on it a third time but I said" don't step there" and I rushed over to her and showed her which stone not to step on.

When I showed her that she stepped over the rock and we continued our journey and then we went through the door in front of us and into the next room.

When we got to the next room we saw that there was a small river of lava that was in the way and then we saw the lever and we knew that there would be keys to find.

So we walked up to the lever to see how many keys we needed and we saw that we needed two and we started looking around and after a long while of hard looking I found the first key(for once).

I put it into the keyhole and turned it and the lava went down halfway and then we started looking for the second key.

We continued looking for a couple of hours but couldn't find it anywhere then I decided to look closer at the ground and that is when I found the second key laying near the entrance.

I picked it up and I put it into the second keyhole and then I pushed it down and the lava went down the rest of the way and we were able to pass through.

So we went past the small empty riverbed that was filled with lava and we went through the door on the other side.

When we got to the other side we saw that we were in a hall but there was a faint light at the end of the hall and when we got to the end of the hallway we saw that we had reached a field and at the edge of the field was a door but this door had one lock on it.

We walked up to the door and started looking for the key and soon found it not too far away and I picked it up and put it into the keyhole and turned it.

When I did the door opened and on the other side was a room that had the chest that we were looking for against the wall.

We walked up to the chest and opened it and inside was the tablet and we waited for the shining to go away and then we looked it over and read it.

The tablet said: go past this door and to the right past the spikes and down the hall and down a waterfall past a three lock door and the fire and ice and you shall find the next note.

At that moment in front of us a door opened and we looked at each other and went through and started walking down the hallway beyond the door.

We continued walking and soon the hallway turned to the right and we could hear the spikes in the distance. After a few moments we came up to the first of the spikes and I noticed that they were in sequence.

So as soon as the first one went down I jumped over it and as I did the second one went down but I knew that it was about to come up again.

So I waited and then I saw it come up again and I went over and then as soon as I went over that one I waited for the last one to go down and when it did I jumped and got over just in time.

Then I motioned for danyelle to start because athero was already on the third one and was about to jump over and then athero jumped over and was standing by me cheering danyelle on.

On the first one she almost lost her balance and then she regained it and then she jumped onto the second one and almost got spiked when she jumped onto the third one but it went down just in time.

We saw that there was a door that was to the right, a door to the left and a door in front of us so we chose the one In front of us.

We started walking and soon we came to a dead end and when we got back to where we were before we made our decision I made a tiny lightning bolt and grabbed onto the end and said "father Zeus show me the way".

When I said that the lightning bolt pointed to the passage to the left and so I disintegrated the lightning bolt and we went down that hall and soon we were walking down a river.

Then I spotted a boat that was floating and seemed to be in better shape than it should be and so we got into it and let the river push us along and then up ahead we saw the waterfall and we knew that we had to go down it.

We braced ourselves and soon we were falling down the waterfall and landed in a pond and we soon saw that the waterfall landed us in a field and at the end of the field was a door that had three locks and we knew that it was the one from the clue.

We went up to it and then I noticed the hole in the ground and I knew that we would have to find a lever as well.

So I started looking for the first part of the lever and when I found the first part it didn't seem like part of a lever at all because it was a small round part and I placed it into the hole and it activated the lever hole.

Then I started looking for the pipe part of the lever and soon I found one part of it laying against a rock and I tried to put it into the hole but it wouldn't fit so I started looking again for the right part because I knew that it was the second or third part of the lever.

Then I found another one and when I put it into my arm the two parts fused and I was looking at the top of the lever and I knew that I had to find the bottom and so I continued looking.

After a few moments I saw the bottom sticking out of the ground and I picked it up and put it with the others and it fused with them and the lever was becoming really difficult to hold and I rushed over to where the levers went and I placed the lever there.

When I did the lever lit up and it started making a humming noise and then I started helping the others find the remaining two keys because they had found one and I could see danyelle holding onto it.

So I walked up to danyelle and she handed the key to me and I put it into the first keyhole and turned it and then I saw a light run down into the lever and I knew that once all the keys were in the lever must be pulled.

Then I started looking for the second key as well as the third one and soon I had found it and I went up to the locks and put the key into the keyhole and turned it and a light went to the lever again.

Then I saw athero coming with the third and final key and we put it into the third keyhole and turned it as well and that light went to the lever again and I went to the lever and pushed it with all my might and soon I had It pushed all the way over and the doors creaked open.

When the doors were open we walked through and found the chest and we opened it and inside was a note that read: don the hall to the right don't go anywhere follow the light it's not far to the tablet in the chest it remains so do your duty or you will be in chains.

We started walking around the room and soon I spotted a light in the corner of the room so I went to it and then it went through the wall so I threw a lightning bolt and broke the wall.

Behind it was a tunnel that led a few feet and I could see a room in the distance and so I started towards the room with the others behind me and soon we were in a small room and inside that small room was a chest and so we went up to it and opened it.

When I did the tablet shined in front of us and we had to cover our eyes until the shine went away and then we looked at it and I started reading and it read: past the chest and down the hall through the mirror and up a flight and down another through some trees and witness mother nature and you will have to find the two keys that stop the nature and you'll find the next note.

As we started at the wall a door appeared and then opened into a hallway and so we went down the hallway and soon we ended up at a dead end and I was about to turn around when I heard a squeal and then a whoosh and the other two were gone.

Then I saw the wall ripple and I knew that the wall was actually a mirror wall and I touched it and it pulled me through and I ended up in another hallway.

In front of me was athero and danyelle and they were motioning for me to come and then when I did we started walking and soon we came to a set of stairs and so we went up and up and up until we couldn't anymore.

Then we started walking down that hallway and then we found another hallway that also had a staircase but this one was also going up and we knew from the tablet that it had to go down.

So we started to go down a different hallway and this one had a staircase that did go down and so we took it and it was a short staircase and when we got off the stairs we noticed that we were on the edge of a field and in the distance was a forest of trees made of stone.

We started for it and then we noticed the smoke and we started to hesitate but then we remembered that we had to witness it to make the door appear.

We continued walking and as we started walking into the forest we soon saw what was making the smoke.

There was lava pouring out of the ground in the midst of the trees and it was starting to cover a good portion of the woods and so we started looking for the lever that would hold the two keys that would stop the lava from covering everything.

So I started looking and after a few hours I sat down on a stump made of stone and I must have sat on a switch because it made the ground open up and reveal the first key.

I started looking for the lever and soon found it by the wall that the lava was getting real close to.

Then I put the key into place and I noticed that there was not one port for the lava to come through but four and that meant that I had to find four keys not two.

So when I put the key into place one of the ports closed and I started looking for the next key and soon found it about to be covered in lava and I picked it up and stepped on a rock in the middle of the lava and put that key into place and when I did the remaining ports closed and I saw the lava quickly residing and I knew now that the clue was right and then there was a slight rumbling and then I noticed that there was a door where there wasn't one before.

So we went up to the door now that the lava was gone and we pushed it open and inside was the chest and we opened it and inside was the note to the third clue and we read it.

It read: down these stairs and through the hall in front of you through the field and through the six lock door and into the room beyond then do the puzzle and you shall get the chest.

When we were done reading the ground opened up and started making stairs and when it was finished we started to go down them into the hallway.

After a few minutes of walking down the hallway we found a door that was wide open and we could see that on the other side was a field.

When we went through it we saw that we were in the field that we needed to be in and we started to have a look around and after a short navigation we located the door that had six locks and we started looking for the keys right away.

We started looking for the keys and then I realized that I had to do the exact same thing that I had to do with the last door and find the lever pieces first.

So while the others were looking for the keys I was looking for the lever pieces and I found the first piece pretty quickly and I put it into the hole and it clicked and I knew that it was the right piece.

So I began to search for the second part and after a few moments of looking I saw it sticking out of the ground so I went to go pull it up and saw that it was a lever to show me where the second lever was.

Every time I would move it a light would shine to a certain spot and I went to that spot and I saw a handle so I pulled it and it was a bunker.

Inside was the second piece of the lever and also the final piece and so I went up to where the lever was and put it with the other one and put it together and it fused and made the lever whole.

Then I started to search for the keys and soon saw that the first key was already found because danyelle had it in her hand and I went up to her and she handed over the key and I went over to the locks and put the first one in the lock and turned it.

Then I started looking for the second key but athero was already heading towards me with it in hand and when he got to me I held out my hand and he handed it over.

I put the second key into the second lock and turned it and It lit up but the first one didn't so I took the first one out and placed it in a different one and I lit up as well.

Then I started to search for the third key and saw athero by the door so I went up to him and I saw that he had the third key and so he handed it over to me and I put it into the third lock but it didn't light up either so I put it in the fifth lock and it lit up as well.

Then we started looking for the fourth key and I quickly found it because it was right beside the door and I put it in the right lock this time because it lit up.

We went back to looking for the keys and soon we found the fifth key and then I put the key into the sixth lock and it lit up and then we started looking for the sixth key and after about a minute I saw it laying on a box in the corner of the small space around the door.

I put the key into the last remaining lock and it lit up and then I pulled the lever and the keys started flashing and then the door swung open.

Inside was grim and then lights turned and we noticed that there was a note in the middle of the floor and so I picked it up and it said: pass my puzzle and you shall get my gold.

Then a pedestal came up from the ground and It looked like a 3d puzzle. I knew exactly who to put to the job and I was about to put athero to the test but he was already there turning knobs and pulling levers.

I was about to sit down when I heard a buzz and then a ding and athero took a bow and almost fell off because the pedestal began to move to reveal steps and once it was done moving I led the way down.

When we got to the bottom we saw the chest in the corner and we went up to it and I opened it to reveal the shine and then once that was gone I picked up the tablet and began to read: go past the door ahead and up the stairs go past the frozen lake and pass the crystals of the u.s. and you shall find the fourth note

As we were reading a door opened behind the chest and the chest sank into the floor and once the floor closed again we started through the door behind it.

We started down the hallway inside and soon we were going up some stairs and after a few minutes of climbing we were all out of breath and we took a breather and then started again and then I noticed something we weren't moving because the stairs were moving down.

So I grabbed the side of the wall and started walking on the wall and then a few minutes later I was at the top of the stairs and the others were still having trouble.

I told them that if they walked on the wall like I did then they would reach the top.

They nodded and started doing what I did and soon they were with me at the top of the stairs and we started again.

When we came out into the open we saw that there was a frozen lake in the center of the room and we walked past it and we continued into the next room.

When we got into the next room we saw that we that we were in a room full of rubies and I walked up to them and started to feel them and then I walked away and we walked into the next room and this room was filled to the brim with sapphires and like the rubies I was drawn to it and I touched it.

When I did the crystal lit up and we began to walk towards the next room but something was telling me to go back to the rubies.

So instead of going to the next room I went back to the ruby room and touched them again and this time when I touched them they lit up as well.

Then I rushed back past the sapphires and into the next room and I saw that the others were already at the diamonds that happen to fill this room.

When I got to them I touched the diamonds and they also lit up and started to shrink revealing a chest and when the crystals were done shrinking I walked up to the chest and opened it.

When we got it open we saw that it held a note and I held the note up and it read: past the crystals of heaven and earth and the seven lock door and beyond that door you will find the fourth clue.

We went through the only door that was an exit and continued down that hallway and soon we came into a room with a whole lot of diamonds and we just kept on walking and then we found another tunnel and soon we were in a room that had another type of crystal in it and I knew that it had to be the earth crystal because it was green as grass.

We started walking again and soon we came upon a field and we started walking and then I noticed the door with seven locks on it and we started down to it.

When we got to it we saw that we just had to get the keys found and put them into the locks.

So we started looking for the first key and soon we had it in hand and I went to put it into the first lock and then I saw the lines around the locks and I knew that it was a light up thing.

So I put the first key into each of the locks but I stopped when the third lock lit up and then I started looking for the second key and after a few minutes athero found it.

Then athero walked up to me and gave it to me to put it into the lock and so I put the key into the lock and it didn't light up so I put it into the others until it lit up.

Then right after I had that one put in, danyelle found the third one and gave it to me to put it in and soon I had it lit up just like the others.

Once I got that one in I started to look for the fourth key and after a few more minutes I found the fourth one and I walked it over to the door and put it into one of the remaining locks but it didn't light up so I pulled it out and put it it the others until it lit up.

By the time I got that one in and lit up she had found the fifth one and was waiting for me to get finished and so I started on the fifth key.

I did the same thing with the fifth key and then started to look for the sixth key and after about an hour we stopped looking and then I saw a glint of gold out of the corner of my eye and keeping my head turned I walked over to where I saw the glint of gold and picked it up and then I turned my head.

When I did I saw that it was the sixth key and I put it into the second to last lock and it lit up and then we started looking for the seventh key.

We soon found the last key inside a barrel and then we put it where it should be. Soon we had all the keys in place and we pulled the lever.

When we did, the door opened and we went inside. Inside was a room that was empty except for a small wooden chest.

we walked up to the chest and opened it and as soon as I opened it there was a blast of bright light and then it faded and we got a good look at the tablet and then I picked it up and read it: down the hall to the right and then another to the left up a flight of stairs and then down another through another mirror and walk on the wall because the floor is liquid nitrogen and if you don't you'll run out of oxygen find the vines with the red flowers and behind those are the note to the fifth clue.

We started looking around but didn't see any tunnels anywhere including the one we came out of and then athero saw one in the dark and we went for it and then I saw one also but we continued on the one that we were going to.

When we got into the tunnel we could barely see our hands in front of our faces and so we continued and then I remembered the torch that I had and I lit it and almost immediately wished I hadn't.

When I did I saw that there were spiders coming from all directions so I quickly gave the torch to athero to hold and I summoned a lightning bolt to my hand and struck the ground with it and everything around us got electrocuted and died.

Then I quickly moved everyone back before anymore came through and then I thought maybe they were guarding something and instead of moving back I moved everyone forwards.

Once we were through the webs we saw the hallway that led to the left and we went to take it and soon we were at the foot of some stairs but they didn't move.

So we started climbing the stairs and soon we were at the top and at the top was a long hallway that curved to the left and then we were at the top of some more stairs going down this time.

We started down these stairs and were soon at the bottom and at the end of the hall I saw the same kind of mirror wall I saw earlier and so I went and motioned for the others to follow me and I went through it to the other side.

When I got to the other side I immediately grabbed the wall because the ground was like a silvery color and I knew that it had to be nitrogen and we couldn't step on it.

We started climbing across the wall and then as we were finally reaching the end we saw that the vines that hide the box that would hold the note to the fifth clue was in sight.

we jumped down at the end of the hallway and went up to the vines and went through them and when we did we saw the chest that would held the note for the fifth clue and we opened it and started to read it and when we did it said: go down that that hall right outside the door watch out quicksand is the floor be quick and nimble on the stones ahead and you'll find that you needn't dread go up two flights and down one and you'll find the gold that was once in a crown.

We went back outside and then I saw the quicksand and I saw where I needed to go to avoid the quicksand and I was off while the other two were contemplating on where to go.

By the time they had figured out where they were going to put their hands and feet I was already halfway across the hallway.

So I finished going across the hall and when I landed I waited for the others to finish and then we started on the next challenge.

When I turned around and saw that there was writing on the wall and it said "who were the three brothers?"

We already knew from our ancestors who the big three brothers were. So we started looking at the floor and it had letters on it and then we looked at each other and wondered "is it really that easy " and then one at a time we spelled out "Zeus, Poseidon, and Hades."

After a few minutes of spelling out those names we reached the other side and then we could see that there were three more questions that we would have to answer.

So we started again once everyone passed the test and once we got to the next question we saw that it was going to be easier from here.

We read the next question which was "who is the king of the gods"? We didn't even have to think for this one and we answered right away because this one didn't have letters and when I answered" zeus" a long road appeared out of thin air.

When I saw that a road appeared I ran across it and motioned for the others to follow and as I did the road disappeared and they had to answer again to make it appear for each person.

Once we were all across that one we saw that there was a door to the left and we started walking slowly down that hall and then we came out into a larger hall and immediately we saw a flight of stairs but this one was going down and so we kept on walking.

We walked a little bit further and soon we came into a slightly bigger room and this room had a staircase going up and so we went up and when we got to the top we started forward and we saw that it had led us to another hallway.

We started walking again and soon we found the next staircase going up and when we reached the top we came to another hallway and we almost fell down the stairs that were at the end of that hallway.

So we started going down but we had to be careful because these stairs were so steep that one wrong move and you would fall to your death.

We finally made it to the bottom and soon we found the chest that held the fifth clue and we opened it and as soon as we did, light flooded the area and we had to cover our eyes.

When the shine cooled down I picked up the tablet and started to read it and it read: against the wall between the two faces you'll find the door with levers on the eyes. Go past that door and swing to the left past the old ruins and through the gates and go across the chasm and you shall find the sixth note.

We started to have a look around the room but there didn't seem to be any faces anywhere, just portraits but those were hanging on the wall and then I noticed that there was one face but it was faded so what if the other was faded as well?

I walked up to the wall and removed the portrait and behind it was a face and I knew that the portrait must have made the face survive when the body couldn't.

I told danyelle to go over to the other face and push the other eye in at the same time as I did and then when we did the wall between them opened up like a door and we immediately turned left and we saw that we would need the torch again so I lit it and we started moving.

After a while of not seeing anything we still had to keep our hopes up and then we ran into some skeletons that looked extremely old and fragile and I knew that it was the old ruins that it had to be talking about.

We stepped over them and we kept on walking and soon we were deep inside the earth and I rose the torch and in the distance I could see the gate but it looked broken down and rusted beyond repair and we just pushed right through that and we just kept on walking and when we did we knew that the chasm had to be somewhere around here.

Then the other two had to pull me back because if they hadn't I would have walked off the edge and perished.

I thanked them and then started to have a look around the premises without going off the edge and then I saw the ledge and how it went all the way around.

I then took a look at the wall and found that you could rock climb it and then I called the others over and we started to climb the wall and when we got to the top we turned to the side and started to make the circular shape that the room was in.

We crawled across the ledge a little at a time and after a few moments of crawling we reached a resting point and we took a rest.

After a few minutes of resting I urged the others to get going if we wanted to make it home by august and we started moving again and that happened a few times and we would have to rest and then we would continue.

When we finally made it to the other end I looked at my clock and saw that it only took us an hour to cross that ledge to get to the other side.

We looked around for the chest and soon we found it in the shadows and we knew that we would have to read it by torch so we lit up the torch and I opened the chest.

When I opened the chest I saw that there was a note that had to be the note for the sixth clue and I picked it up and read it: go down the slide right into the wealthy and into a world where everyone you want is healthy go past that door and go to the one on the right bring a torch because it won't have light go into the last room on the right and up the stairs and down that hall and after that heed the call.

We started to move the chest and when we got it moved we saw that there was a slide that it was covering and so we went down the slide and at the bottom was a hallway and that hallway had three doors two on the left and one on the right.

We walked past the two doors on the left and started through the one on the right and as soon as I did the torch went out but we didn't need it because this room had some kind of light inside of it and it made it to where we didn't need the torch anymore.

We looked around for some stairs and after a few moments we found them and then we went down the hall and we then heard a buzzing and the tablet from the last clue flew to my hand and started to guide me.

We went through a wall that seemed solid and past a statue of zeus and then one of Heracles and then it led us to a field and then it got out of my hand and started flying towards a door and this door had four locks and two levers that had to be found.

So we started looking meanwhile the tablet just stuck to the door like a magnet to a fridge and I told them to look for the keys and I would look for the lever pieces.

They nodded and soon I found a diamond as large as my hand and then I put it into my pocket and I went back to looking for the lever pieces and as soon as I had started to look the others gave me a key.

I had no choice but to stop searching for the lever and put the key into place. When I had that done I started to search for the first part of the lever and soon found it laying in plain sight.

Then I put the first part of the lever into the hole and it clicked and we started looking again and then I found the second part of the second lever but I was looking for the second part of the first lever or the first part of the second lever.

So I held onto the piece that I had just found and started looking again and soon I found another piece and danyelle gave me another key and so I went to the door.

When I went to the door I put the key into place first and then I tried to figure it out I had a whole lever or three quarters of one.

After a few moments I finally figured it out and the first and second pieces of the second lever fused together and I put them into the ground where they would go.

Then I started looking for the last piece of the first lever and the last piece of the second lever and after a few moments of searching I found the diamond for the second lever and I went over to it and screwed it on and it began to shine and then it dimmed.

Then I started to search again and shortly after athero came up to me and handed me another key and as he was handing it to me I looked down and there was the last lever piece.

I picked it up and I went back to the door where the tablet was still stuck to the door and put the last part of the lever in its place and the third key in its place and then I walked up to danyelle and asked if she wanted any help but she just shook her head and I just walked back to the door.

As soon as I sat down she came walking up with the key in hand and she offered the key to me and I took it and I went ahead and put the key into its place and then the door swung open.

When it did the tablet flew into the room and then flew straight down into a hole.

We looked down into the hole and in it was the chest and we knew that it had to hold the sixth tablet and we opened it and a shining appeared as usual and when it dimmed I picked up the tablet and read it and it read: go through the door up ahead and past the room that was filled with old lava and through the hole in the water to the other side and through the Indian arch and the room on the other side and you will find the seventh tablets note.

While we were reading a door started to appear and when we looked up we looked around and I was the first one to spot it and I went up to it and said" this wasn't here earlier was it" then the other two shook their heads and I went to open the door but found out that it didn't have a handle so I started to search for a way to get it open and then I saw the crack in the center and I knew that it opened in half and I pulled the middle of the door and more light started to appear until I got it open and the light dimmed and we started down that hallway.

We continued walking until we started to see doorways but they didn't have doors on them and the first one was empty and so was the second one but the third was filled with brimstone and I knew that because it smelled like a fart.

We went past that room in a hurry and went to the next hallway and I led to a large room that had a lake In the middle of it and I knew what we had to do and so we went into the water and dove under and in the center was a hole the size of a car and we started towards it.

We started swimming through it and once we got to the hole we noticed just how big it was and we started swimming to the surface of the water until we breached.

Once we got our lungs full of air again we dove again and went straight down and managed to make it all the way through the hole to the other side.

When we got to the other side we started towards the shore and we went to dry off but to our amazement we were already dry.

We started walking again and soon we were in a cave with drawings on the walls and I knew that we had to be close to the Indian arch and so we started again and soon we came into another room that held a bunch of Indian artifacts.

In front of us was the holy grail of Indian artifacts: the Indian arch and we went through it and when we did a door opened on the other side and we went through it and on the other side was the chest and so we went up to it and opened it to reveal the note to the seventh clue.

When we picked the chest closed and I got the note out just in the nick of time.

When I got the note out I immediately began to read it and it read: go down this hallway to the right and up the stairs and down a flight past the waterfall that looks like lava and then go through the entrance that is through the door go past the lava that looks like a waterfall go into the cave behind the lava and you will have what you seek.

While we were reading a door appeared and I was the first one to go to the door and I opened it and soon I was going through it and started to go up the hallway and then after a few minutes of walking the tunnel turned to the right.

When we turned the corner we saw that it ended up in a room and this room was enormous and in the middle was a flight of stairs and so we started to climb the stairs and soon we were at the top.

At the top was a long hallway that curved to the right and we continued walking until it ended in another set of stairs and we started to climb down carefully and once we were back on safe ground we started again and we decided to have a look around and after a few moments we found another hallway and then we started down that hallway and after a few minutes we came out into a field.

In the field was a waterfall that was red like lava and we continued forward and then we saw the door and this one looked like it had locks on it but when we got a better look we saw that the locks were already done.

We went through it and soon we saw that we were in an old room that we had already done but there was a door that we didn't see before.

We went through that door and soon we were in a different room that was a bit smaller and we went into the door on the left wall and found ourselves in another field.

At the edge of the field there was a waterfall that was nothing but lava.

After a long hike of twenty minutes we got there but we had to watch our step and then we remembered that we had to go behind the lava.

so we started towards the waterfall part and started to climb behind it. When I did the lava almost splashed me a few times and then we reached the cave and we were relieved to be away from that lava and we started looking for the tablet and we saw a chest in the center of the back wall and so we went up to it.

When we did we saw that it was empty and then we saw another chest and we knew that this one had to be the right one.

We went up to it and opened it and there was a brilliant light that we had to cover our eyes and when I shimmered down we saw that the tablet was in that chest.

I picked up the tablet and I noticed that this one was a bit different because it didn't have any words on it.

When I picked it up however it started to form words and when the words were down forming I read: go through the hole and down the stairs and follow the hall but needn't dare, go down the hallway and past the crystal fireworks and you shall find the eighth clues note.

We started looking for a hole in the ground but couldn't find one for a few minutes and then I lit a torch and then I saw a circular pattern in the floor and I knew that it had to be the hole in the floor.

So we found the handles which was pretty easy and soon we were pulling the circular piece out of place and under it was a hole in the ground and I could see a rope that didn't look old to me hanging from the hole.

I got onto the rope and jerked on it a few times and it seemed steady and so I climbed onto it and started down and by the time I was on the ground below danyelle was halfway down the rope as well.

Then all that was left was athero and he pretty much just fell the last twenty feet or so.

We rushed over to him and went to see if he was okay and when he nodded we started down the stairs that were in front of us.

While we were going down the stairs we started to hear rumbling and then I saw two big boulders coming right for us.

We barely reached the bottom of the stairs on time and dodge the boulders then they smacked into the wall and made a hole in the wall.

We went through the wall and into the next room but there wasn't anything there so we walked through the door across the room and that door led us to a hallway.

We walked down that hallway and soon found ourselves in another room that was almost identical to the one we were just in except for the fact that it had gold piled in a corner.

We started toward another hallway and this one ended in a circular room with a pedestal that had three holes in the top and the room also had three doors in front of us.

We started with the first one and when we got to the room we saw that it had rubies in it and on a desk there was a single ruby on it.

I immediately knew what I had to do with that one and I picked it up and we walked back to the last room that we were in and I placed the ruby in the first spot where there was a red outline.

Then we went into the second room and it was filled with diamonds and like the first one it had a single diamond on a desk and so I picked it up.

Then I carried it over to the pedestal and put it into the third spot because that was where the white outline was.

Then we went into the last room and this one was filled with sapphires with a single sapphire chunk laying on the table so I picked it up and we went back to the pedestal and put it into the last hole.

Then three lights lit up and a door began to open to the right of us and we went through to find the chest that the eighth note to the eighth clue would be in and we opened the chest and saw the piece of paper inside and so we picked it up and read it: through the secret passageway and down the hall through the north quarters and through the field and open the four door two lever door and you shall find the eighth clue.

As we were reading a door began to form and we knew from instinct that we would have to go through that one.

Once it was done forming we opened it and started down the hallway inside and as we continued down the hallway we noticed that the walls were beginning to change color from brick to limestone.

When we finally got down that long hallway we saw that the exit was a room and I assumed that this was the north quarters and so we continued on down the path that we were on.

When we got into the room where the north quarters were we didn't see an exit so we started looking around and soon I moved a box to the side and saw a hole that we could crawl through.

Once we got through that hole we found ourselves in a field that was almost like it was above ground.

When we got into the field we saw the door at the far end of the field so we started towards it and when we got to it we started looking for it and I said to the others" once again I'll look for the lever pieces while you look for the keys."

They nodded and went to work trying to find the keys and meanwhile I saw a brilliant light out of the corner of my eye and I walked up to it and it was a ruby.

So I walked around trying to find the pieces to the lever and it took awhile to find the other gem to the other lever.

Before I could find any of the actual pieces to the levers athero walked up to me and handed me the first key and I walked up to the door and I put it into the first lock and turned.

Then I turned around and danyelle was right up on me and she handed me a key as well and I put it into the third lock and it also clicked as it turned.

Then I started looking for the levers again before they could bother me again.

I looked around the door and then after a few minutes of looking I started looking around the hole that we had just gone through and I saw something sticking out of the ground and I picked it up and saw that it had a screwy end.

I pulled out the ruby and screwed it one and then I knew that it was the top of the lever and I started looking for the bottom of it.

When I looked down I saw that there were four arrows and one was pointing to where the first part of the lever was found so I started moving in the direction of the second arrow and soon I found the second part of the first lever and I put it together and I had the first lever.

I put it into the hole and pulled and the first two keys lit up and started turning even more and the top half opened.

Then I started looking again but I had to find that marking first so I started looking for that marking and soon found it.

I mentally crossed out the two arrows that pointed to where the ones that I had already found were so I went to where one of the other two arrows were pointing and soon I had found the top of the second lever and I screwed the lever in and started looking again.

Then I followed the final arrow to the last piece of the lever and soon I had the other lever put together and then I felt a tap on my shoulder and behind me was danyelle and athero.

When I was about to ask what they wanted they handed out their keys and I knew exactly what they wanted and that is for me to put the keys in.

So I put my lever on it but didn't push it over and then I put my skills to good use and put the keys into their place and turned them and then I pushed the lever and the keys turned even more and the bottom opened.

When the door was all the way open we went through and saw that we were in a huge room that had a chest against the wall and we knew that it had to be the one that we were looking for.

So we started walking up to it, opened it and when I did there was a bright light as always and then as usual it dimmed.

I reached into the chest and pulled out the tablet and I read the tablet: go through the door in front of you and if you don't you'll go down the steps and down the hall and turn but go past the hall and into the next room and you will find what is related to you.

As we were reading we saw a door opening and we knew from experience that we had to go through that door and almost immediately afterwards we found the steps and almost fell down them.

I fell down one step and then caught myself and then warned everyone else and then we started down the steps and soon we were at the bottom.

When we reached the bottom we started down the hallway in front of us and when we got there we saw that we were in a hall full of doors and one of them lay open.

I walked up to it and saw that it was a hallway that we could go down and then I remembered what the clue had said and passed it up.

When we finally got to the end of the tunnel type hallway we came into this room and we saw this chest in the corner and we knew that it had to be the chest with the note inside.

I picked it up and read it: go through the mirror and it will transport you to the next part, go past the lake and the fire and you will need to find the three pieces of the triangle and to do that you will have to pull three levers and that will find you to the ninth clue

We walked around and as I did I was feeling the wall and then my hand went through it and I knew that it was the mirror wall and so I walked back to where the wall was and went through and I went through.

When I came out the other side I saw that I was in another room and this room was different from the last one.

Once we were all on the same side of the wall we started moving again and soon we were in the next room and we saw that there was a huge lake in the middle of it.

We walked past the huge lake and saw that there was something swimming in it and we rushed past that because we didn't want to have anything to do with it.

Then as we walked into the next room we saw that there was a chasm and then as the others were trying to figure out how we were going to get across the fire I yelled at them and they turned around.

When they did I showed them the door to the left of the door that we had just come out of.

We walked through that door and when we did we noticed that up ahead we could see that there weren't any flames in sight.

We walked across that room and soon we were on the other side and on the other side was a pedestal and above the door was a large three part triangle.

I then noticed that there were three doors and I knew that there was at least one triangle piece in each door.

So I went into the first door and found the first lever right away because it wasn't hidden at all so I started looking for the second lever and had to actually look for that one but after a few minutes I stopped looking and started feeling the wall.

The wall looked solid but I could fall through at any second and that is exactly what happened right then and I saw stars because I clipped my head on the lever and

When the stars cleared up I realized what I had found and I pulled the lever.

After I pulled that lever I started to search for the final lever of the first triangle and after a while of walking around I found the final lever.

When I found the final lever I pulled that one as well and started walking back and when I got back I saw that there was a triangle part sticking out of the side of the pedestal.

So I grabbed it and put it in the top right part of the triangle and started to search for the first lever of the second triangle.

At that time danyelle came out of nowhere holding the second triangle piece and she put it into the bottom of the triangle.

That only left us one thing left for us to find so we started looking for the third triangle levers.

We started at one end of the room and then went up and down the hallway. Then when we had looked just about everywhere we were heading back and I was feeling the wall in the main part when I fell through and found the three levers.

When I found the levers I pulled them all at the same time and then we went back to the pedestal and the third part of the triangle was hanging from the side.

We put the last piece of the triangle in its place and it glowed green and then we heard a rumble.

Then the ground opened up in front of us and the chest lifted out of the ground on its own stage.

So we went around the pedestal and up to the chest and saw that it was a silver color and we knew that it had to be the second to last tablet.

I opened it and as soon as I did I got a blast of silver light which was different from that of the rest.

When the light finally faded we saw that we were looking at a silver tablet and I picked it up and read it: go down the hall and to the right up the stairs and down a flight go past the door with the six lock gate and soon you will seal your fate.

When we were done reading we stopped for a second and pondered for a moment on what it could mean and then we heard a grinding noise and a door opened to the left.

We looked at each other and then we went through the door and soon we were in a hallway that seemed to curve to the right.

We kept walking and then the hallway began to narrow and then we started to go up and I noticed that we were on some stairs and we leveled out.

Then we started to go down and then after a few minutes of doing that we leveled out again and we could see light pouring in from ahead.

We burst into the light and we saw that we were in a field and at the edge was a gate that had six locks on it so nothing new.

We walked up to it and looked at the locks and we noticed that they had a specific pattern.

Then we started looking for the keys that would open the locks and after a few minutes I found the first one by the entrance.

When I found it I went up to the locks and I noticed that the key had a certain type of swirl on it and so did the locks so I matched the key with the lock.

I had to put that one into place as well.

Then the door swung open and we went through it and inside was a room that was dusty and there at the wall to the side was a chest that was really old looking and we knew that it had to hold the note to the second piece of Poseidon's trident.

We opened it and saw that it was empty so we started searching the room and saw another chest in a chair where a skeleton was sitting so we pulled the box off the skeletons lap and opened it and inside was the note to the second piece of the trident.

I picked up the note and I read it: go past the river and through the door that is see through and then go through the wall that can give you millions and you shall find the staff part of the trident of poseidon.

As we were reading a door opened to the right and so we knew that we had to go through it and when we did we found ourselves in a hallway that wasn't very long.

Then we came into a room with a river in it (or what used to be a river).

I walked to the edge of the river and then I noticed that the river moved out of the way as I got closer and then I called the others to me.

When they got to where I was I walked out towards the river and it moved out of the way and so I continued and then I motioned for the others to follow as I went across.

Then as I got across I stood at the edge of the water until the others had made it across and then we started walking again.

After we had gone across the river we started across the room and ducked through a hole in the wall and on the other side of the wall was another hallway.

We walked down that hallway until we coming to a part of it that had some doors and we noticed that none of them were see through so we just kept on going until we were in front if a rock wall and we knew that we had to go through and the only way that we could do that was to touch it.

We reached out at the same time and we were sucked in as usual and we landed on dry ground on the other side but we didn't fall this time.

When we landed we got up and looked behind us to see another dead end wall and then we looked in front of us and saw that there was a door that was in the far wall.

From the looks of it this was the see through door and we went up to it and I reached out to it and then I walked through when I saw that it didn't do anything to you when it touched you.

As a matter of fact it was just like any other door because there was a room on the other side of the door and we started to have a look around and that is when we noticed a little stretch of wall that was made of gold bricks.

We walked up to it and we each took a stance and touched the wall at the same time and we vaporized through the wall (seriously).

We took a look around and saw a glowing staff above on a shelf but before we could get to it rocks started to come down.

We began to cover our heads but then I looked up and I saw that there was an electricity shield over us and then I noticed that I was making it.

Once the rocks were done falling I summoned an electric staff and started to hammer through them.

After a few minutes we finally broke through the last of the boulders and we went up to the shelf and we grabbed the staff and put it into the bottom of the last piece we found.

When we did they began to mold together and we knew that there was only three more places to go and then rolled the marbles that chiron had gave to us before we had departed and said "titicaca" and then they rolled and hit the far wall and together they made a portal and we visualized the peru's lush landscape and we were confused when we were on the edge of a lake.

{ four }

Peru

Then I walked up to the lake and for some reason this water started to part as well and then I remembered that I still had the last tablet from the last place.

So I pulled it out and I saw that there must be a reason that this worked here and I saw that there was a peninsula and so I went down the peninsula and held out the tablet and saw nothing but mud and then after a few moments I saw a road that was partially covered in mud.

Then as I walked on the road I held the tablet out in front of me and then I saw what looked like an old well that had been covered and I walked over to it and uncovered it and then I saw that it had a ladder leading down and I knew that it had to be our way in.

I climbed over the edge after motioning for the others to follow me and as we were going down we heard cracks and drops of water falling and then the ladder that we were climbing down on broke and we fell the last two feet right onto the bare ground that was a little muddy.

When we got up we started to have a look around and we saw that there was a small tunnel leading away from the so we started going down that tunnel and when we were going down that tunnel we noticed that the rock started to change from clay to limestone and we knew that we were going down.

When the tunnel ended we found ourselves in another room and this one was full of wonders (like for example there was a waterfall that shined like it was made from crystals.

Then I looked above the waterfall and I saw that words started to form and they read: through this waterfall and down this road cross the river and you shall reach the two lock two lever door and that is where you will find the first clue.

As we were reading the room began to fill with water.

Once we got through reading we knew that we had to go through that waterfall as fast as we could so we went to go through the waterfall but instead found ourselves swimming.

We started towards the waterfall but it was going so hard that it was impossible to go through and so we started looking for a way through and then danyelle said" hey guys come in the side it's a lot safer"

Then she showed us where she had come into the side of the waterfall and we went through ourselves.

When we were all through the waterfall we started walking again and soon we were back where we started with the water to our chest now so we started a different approach and took another look around in the hallway.

That is when we saw the second tunnel to the right and so we went for that tunnel and soon we came out in another room and that room had a thick river running through it that we had to cross.

I immediately started to look for levers and saw something in the corner and so I went up to it and I saw that it was a lever but it was pushed into the ground.

I tried to pull it up but it wouldn't budge and then I heard danyelle say" Zack there is a button over here that I think goes with that lever, right athero "?

Athero shrugged his shoulders and grinned and then I walked over to them and pushed the button and there was a buzzing and then a click and I saw the lever spring up.

I walked up to the lever and pulled it and at that moment I saw the grips and as I was pulling it wasn't going anywhere and when I changed the way my hands were and pulled it started to come further towards me until it was all the way down.

Once it was all the way down the river began to slow and then it stopped completely and we knew that we had minutes if not seconds before it started to go again.

So we hurried across and as soon as we were about half way the river started running again and then as we waded to the other side the full on rush of the river came back.

We continued walking and soon we came across a field and we walked across the field and on the far side was the door that we had to go through but the levers were nowhere to be found.

We started to look around and then I saw where the levers were supposed to go.

As we were looking for the keys I was put in charge of finding the levers and I told them to leave me alone with the keys to just put them in the keyholes when they found them.

It wasn't long before I found the first half of the first lever and I walked up to the door and put it into the lever part that was right beside the door.

After I put the part of the lever where it was supposed to be I started looking again and soon I had found the second part of the same lever and I put it with the last one and fused them together.

I went back to looking and soon I had found the first part of the second lever and I put it right next to the first one and put it in it's hole and then we started looking again and not long after I was looking I found the last part of the last lever and fused it to the first part.

When I did I saw that they had been waiting for me to find the last lever and the door opened when I did and we went through it into a cobwebbed room.

We walked around the room and soon I had found the chest and I went up to it and saw that it had the trident on it and I knew that we were in the right spot.

I opened it and had to cover my eyes and when the glare lifted off we looked down and saw that there was a tablet inside and had to turn around to the other two and tell them to stop arguing about who is going to read the tablet and at that moment I picked it up and told the others to be quiet and we read:go past the red white and blue, through the crystal blue and up on the other side of the water you will come out of and you will find a chest with a trident on it that is your cue, open it up and you will find the second note to the second clue.

We heard a rumbling and turned to the left and saw that a door was opening and we went through it to find that we were in a room full of rubies and we walked up to the rubies and then I noticed that there was a huge ruby plate and I could see it move.

When I saw that I knew not to touch it because it would suck us in if we touched it.

So we continued moving and soon we were in a room with diamonds in it and I saw that it had a plate as well and I knew that the sapphire one would be the one that we would have to go through and we continued moving.

We went through the door expecting the sapphire room to be the next room over but the next room over was bare except for a few boxes.

We went into the next room to find that it was empty like the last one and then we saw a shimmer in the corner through a door and so we went through that door but it wasn't the sapphire stones instead there was a underground lake and it was making shimmers coming off it's surface.

We went through the other side of the room that the lake was in and immediately found the sapphires and this room didn't have a plate made of sapphires.

So we started to have a look around In the little room that we were in and saw that one of the crystals was a lot bigger than the rest and then I walked up to it and held my breath.

Then I walked through it into the water. I turned around to see the others follow through behind me and we saw the surface and as soon as we broke it we headed for shore.

When we got onto shore I saw that we were in another part of the cave and this part had lots of boxes and a few chests but only one of them had a trident and so I opened it and it had a note in it and I read it and it read: go down that hall to the right and up the stairs and hold tight slide down the other side and go down that hall and you shall find the second clue.

We started towards the hallway that it had mentioned and as soon as we got to it we saw a shadow out of the corner of our eyes and we knew that they had to be hell hounds so we started running and then we heard howling and that only made us run faster.

We looked back and saw that we had lost them and then we turned around only to find ourselves face to face with them.

As a scared demigod I summoned a lightning bolt out of thin air and threw it at the darn thing and it hit it dead on and it fried it to pieces.

Then we started walking again and started down the hall again and we found the right that we were supposed to take and then we continued to walk that path and as we did we saw that there were many doorways and only one led to stairs so we went through that one.

When we did we came out into a room that was way too majestic for this setting and we started up the stairs and as we were climbing we saw that it was a long way down and we started to climb again and decided not to look down again.

Once we got to the top we wiped our heads and then after a few minutes of breaking time we started again and we were well rested.

Once we got to the end of the hallway we saw that there was a slide to the bottom and we knew that we had to slide to the bottom so we started looking for something to slide down on.

After a few moments almost everybody had found something except me and I was still looking so I opened one of the two doors that I had just realized were there at the top of the staircase and Inside was a bed so I grabbed the slab.

When I went to put it on the slide it went without me so I had to find something else and so I looked in the other room and saw a piece of metal and I picked that up and sat on it that way it didn't go without me then I scooted forward and I flew to the bottom where I ran into the wall.

We started down the hall and found a room but it was a small one and it didn't have any boxes at all or chests all it had in it was a small hole in the wall that had a shelf.

On the shelf was a jewelry box and we knew that it wasn't going to be in there but we checked in there anyway.

We opened the jewelry box and inside was a key and then I turned around and saw that there was a keyhole in the ground but I could barely see it.

When I put the key into the keyhole it opened up and inside was a chest that was silver and I jumped down into the hole and picked up the chest and put it on level ground.

Once it was on level ground I opened it and we had to cover our eyes until the shine went away and then I picked it up and read it: go down the hall and past the river that needs four levers to cross and you shall not pass until you find the hidden cross and the room on the far end of the hallway past that room is where you will find the third note to the third clue.

At that we saw a door open to the right of us and we started walking but as we started to get closer we saw that the door was closing.

So we hurried up and went through that door and once we were through that door and in the hall we started walking down the hallway in front of us.

As we were walking I noticed that we were going even deeper into the ground because the rock turned from limestone to the kind of rock that the continental shelf was on.

We were walking about maybe forty minutes and then we began to see light and then we walked into a room that had a mighty river running through it and it was even mightier than that of the last one.

Then I looked around and saw that there were four flat rocks in a row and I knew that if we stood on them they would bring something up and then I remembered that there were four and only three of us.

So I started looking around and saw a large rock in the corner and I tried to pick it up and found out that it was connected to the wall so I summoned a lightning bolt and it blasted right through the rock and I yanked it free.

I began to carry the rock over to the extra stone and I put it onto the stone and we got onto the last three and when we did the ground opened up and revealed the levers.

The first thing I noticed about the levers was there were a couple of keys for all four of the levers so there were eight keys we had to find to pull the four levers.

So we started looking and soon we had the first key and I put it in the first lever because the second thing I noticed was each lever had a particular pattern and the key matched it.

So we started looking for the next key and after a few moments I saw a rusty little piece of metal and I picked it up and I saw that it was another key but this one didn't belong to the first lever it belonged to the third one so I brought it to it and put it in and continued searching.

A few minutes and a half later we heard athero coming and he placed a key in my hand and I looked over the pattern and saw that

It matched the second one so I put the key into that one and then we continued looking.

Then an hour passed and we didn't find a thing and then all of a sudden I saw two at once and I picked them up and I saw that one was to the fourth one and the other was the other one to the third one.

So I went to the third one first and the lever began to light up and I motioned for danyelle to come to me and then I pointed to the lever and had her stand on the rock.

When we did the lever began to go down and then part of an iron blockage started to go across the river.

So we started looking again and then athero and I found two more keys at the same time and he came over to me and handed them to me.

We put the one that I found in the fourth lever and as I did the lever went down and then the iron blockage went farther across.

Then we put the one that Athero had found in the second one and then I had athero stand on that one and it began to go down and I went in search for the last key and soon found it where the rock was and I knew that the rock was supposed to be hiding it.

I picked it up and went to the last lever and put it in as I was standing on it and as I did it went down and the iron blockage stopped the water all together.

We started walking across the place where the water used to be and then the water started to overflow and we knew that we didn't have long.

We rushed across to the other side and as soon as we were across the water began to overflow so much that the blockage wasn't much help.

We started walking again and soon we were in another hallway and we saw that the hallway ended in a door and as we got near the door we saw that it didn't have a handle.

We walked up to it and I put my hand up to it and tried to feel for a handle but my hand went right through the door and then I went through and on the other side was a room and inside was a chest with a trident on it and we walked up to it and I opened it and we peered inside.

Inside was a scroll and I picked it up and I unrolled it and it read: go past this door and down the hall and past the hardest metal on earth and the hardest mineral on earth and you will find the third clue.

As we were reading we saw a door start to open and when we looked up from the scroll there was a door to the left of us and we went through it and came out in a hallway.

We continued down this hallway until we saw that there was a brilliant light up ahead and we kept on going to find ourselves in a room with a clear gem and we thought to ourselves" what is the hardest mineral on earth" and then we came up with the answer" diamonds".

We looked around and we saw that we were in a room full of diamonds and we knew that this was what the scroll meant and we started walking again.

Soon we were walking down a hallway that was laden with gold and I knew that the hardest metal on earth was titanium and we continued after grabbing some gold for the road.

Once we got some gold we started walking again and soon we came across a slick streak that was a silver color but we didn't think that it would be silver.

So we started walking again and pretty soon we were in another one of those doors and I went through it to find myself in another room and in a corner was a chest and it was a gold color and so we went right up to it and I opened it.

When I did I covered my eyes because of the glare on the tablet.

Once the glare was gone I picked up the tablet and read the clue and it read: go through the door in the chest and down the hall beneath past the green and through the seven locked door and a four lock door and you shall find the note for the fourth clue.

When we got done reading we saw that the chest had a string attached to the bottom and so I pulled it and it opened to a ladder going down.

I stepped onto the ladder and started going down and then I motioned for the others to follow and once I got further down the ladder they got onto the ladder themselves.

Once we were near the bottom the ladder seemed to just end and then I put my foot on a rung that was invisible and we just kept on going.

When we got to the bottom we started down the hallway and after about an hour of walking we were starting to feel tired and we knew that there was what doctors call laughing gas in this hallway but there wasn't enough to make us fall asleep just make us tired.

We continued walking and after a few minutes we started to gain mental capability again.

We started down the hall again and soon we came out into a field and I didn't think that it was the green that It meant.

Then I looked around and saw that there weren't any doors either so we started looking for another hallway and then I barely spotted one that was in the dark and we went through the field and went into the hall that that door led into.

We continued on our way and soon we came to a room and it had emeralds In it and we saw a door leading out on the other side of the room.

We went through that door and it led to a tunnel that was a tad bit darker but we could still see and we took that passageway and soon we were in another field.

We looked around that field and after a few good minutes of looking we located the first door and we saw that it had four keys.

We started looking and soon found the first one out of four and this time they didn't pattern on them instead they had roman numerals on them and this one had a three on it.

I put the key into the third lock and then turned it and It clicked and then we started looking for the second key and we found it by the door half way in the ground.

Once we found the second key I put that key into the lock and when I did it clicked and we started to search for the third one and danyelle soon found it and handed it over to me.

When I had the key I put it into the lock and when I did the lock clicked and I saw that we only had one left.

We started searching top to bottom but the key wasn't in sight and we just knew that there was something that we had to do and then athero sat on a nearby rock and then the rock began to sink.

When the rock was sinking a door was opening under me and we saw that inside was a box and the key.

I went into the hole and pulled out the key and put it into the last remaining lock and as soon as I put it in the door began to open enough for us to pass.

When we got through that door we found ourselves in a room and we knew that we had to find another door and after a few minutes we found it but one of the keys was already found and the lock opened.

We knew that we had to find the remaining six keys and so we started looking again but in a new area.

We found the first one on a barrel in a corner but had to move some papers to get to it and then I put the key in the lock and turned it.

When I did it clicked and we started to search for the next one and shortly after we found the first one we found the second one in a box right beside it.

I opened the box and then when I had got the key out of the box I put the second key into the lock and turned it and it clicked.

Once we got the second key we began to search for the third one and within minutes athero had found the third one and he walked over and handed over the key and then I went over to the door and put it into the lock.

Then we started looking for the fourth one and soon we had found that one as well and then before I could put the fourth one in the lock that it belonged to, danyelle gave me the fifth key and I put them both in the last two locks.

Once I had all the locks unlocked the door opened and we went through it and found ourselves in a room that was quite dusty and in the corner was a box.

I walked up to it and I saw that it had a trident on the side and I went to open it and then I called the others over and then I opened it and inside was a scroll and I picked it up and read:through this passage you will find the clue but there is two things you must do first you must pass the veil of eternity and second you must pass the chasm of death and you will find the clue.

We started walking again and soon we found ourselves in a room that had an archway In the middle of it and we walked up to it and when we got up close we saw that it said "the veil of eternity".

We walked through it and nothing happened so I guessed that we had passed that test and we just kept on walking and went into the hallway on the other side and after a few minutes of walking we came out on the other side.

When we got out of the hallway we saw the chasm of death in front of us and then I took a leap of faith and to my relief my foot landed on stone.

I looked down and saw that there was a rock road going across that blended in with the surroundings and if you wanted to get across then you had to take a leap of faith.

Once we got to the other side we saw the chest that would hold the fourth clue and we walked up to it, opened it and had to cover our eyes until the light dimmed and then I picked it up and read it and

It said: go through this door by the hand and pass through the last stand. Go through the doors of nine and you shall be at note number five.

Once we got done reading the tablet a black door came rising out of the ground and then a thick film sort of substance poured onto its surface as we watched.

I went up to it and reached out my hand and closed my eyes but before I could touch it the film grabbed me and pulled me in and when I opened my eyes again I was on the other side of the film and I hoped that the others wouldn't chicken out and come through after me.

After a few minutes had passed I began to get worried and then I started to walk away and then I heard the others land with a bunch of poof's and squeals.

Once they got over themselves they saw me and ran over to give me a hug and then we started on our way.

After a few minutes we were in a skeleton graveyard and we knew that this had to be the last stand and we saw the door on the other side so we started walking towards it and then we saw that it was beginning to close and we barely got through it and on the other side was a door and it had two levers so I put athero to work getting them pulled down as I got a good look around.

That is when I noticed the key hanging from a thread so I began to look for a way to get it and then I saw a ledge and then I began to climb and after a few minutes I got to the ledge.

I jumped off the ledge because it wasn't as high as the last ones that we had been on and I grabbed the key and found out that it was a mirage then I heard a click and the first door opened as the ground was breaking out from under our feet.

We ran towards the exit and as

The ground was going out from under us and we jumped into the next room and landed hard on the solid ground.

We got up and saw that there was another door in front of us and it was open as were the next five and we could see the eighth door so we walked past door two, three, four,five,six, and seven.

Then we started working on the eighth one only to find that it was already unlocked.

So we pushed it open and we started walking towards the last door and this one was locked with two keys and when we saw the locks danyelle smiled because she knew what we had to do.

We all did so we started looking for the keys and right as soon as we did we had found the key that went to the first lock because it had a swirly one on it and I put it into the lock and turned it.

Then I started looking for the last key and after a few minutes of what we started to think that we were not going to find it and then I noticed the shiny bit of silver sticking out of the ground so I went over and pulled it out of the ground and saw that it was the last key.

I cleaned it off and put it into the last lock and turned it and the ninth door opened into a large room and it was filled to the brim with boxes.

We started looking for something that would have a note for us in it and after a few moments of looking I saw an old box that didn't look like it belonged so I went up to it and opened it.

When I did I saw a piece of paper at the bottom of the box and then the others came over and we read it together: go past the diamond gates and through the gates made of diamonds and rubies and then pass through the barrier and you shall find the fifth clue.

We started walking and after a while we came to a hallway that led three ways so we started by going the left way but it led right back to where we were in a tunnel that we had missed.

So we went into the tunnel to the right and It must have merged with the first tunnel because we came back out the exact same tunnel that we had come out of the first time so we went into the only tunnel left of the center tunnel that we must have crossed over last time.

We continued down that tunnel until we came across a rusty old gate and we thought that we had made another wrong turn until athero pointed at a sign and said" look it says the diamond gates."

Then we started walking again and we found ourselves in another hallway that was almost identical to the last one except for the fact that there was only one hallway this time and then we started walking and I noticed that the walls began to change again from the color that they were to a dark brown and I knew that we must be going up again.

Then we started to go down again and we turned a corner and the hallway curved to the left and up ahead we could see a shining gate that seemed to be made of diamonds and rubies and as we walked up to it we saw that it was already open and we walked through it and left it behind and kept on walking down that hallway and when we thought that we couldn't walk anymore we came onto a brick wall and I knew what I had to do was touch it and I would get sucked through.

I reached out my hand and as soon as my palm was flat as a pancake on the wall, I was pulled through the wall and the others followed suit.

Then once we were on the other side we saw the chest that we knew would have the fifth clue in it and so we went up to it and I tried to lift the lid but it was too heavy.

So I summoned the others over to help me out and with all of our strength together we got the lid open and had to immediately shield our eyes from the clue.

When the light died down a bit I picked up the tablet and read it: go down the hall and into the water and onto the other side and down that hall and pull the lever of the cat that is inside and you will find the note to the sixth clue.

We started walking and we saw a hallway up ahead and when we got up to it we started walking down that hallway for awhile until we came into a room that had a enormous pond on the edge of the room and so we walked up to the pond and started into it as you would any other body of water and then dove down.

When we got under the water we saw that there was a small hole in the bottom and we had to go through that hole and as we were going through that hole we noticed that we were almost out of breath by the time that we were on the other side.

We almost didn't make it to the surface in time because I for one was out of oxygen by the time I was through the hole.

When we finally got to the other side we climbed out of the water and laid on the shore for a few moments and looked up at the cave ceiling.

We rested there for a while and then one by one we got up and we started towards the door.

We went down the hallway and saw glittering in the corner and we decided to make a detour and we turned left and went to look at the diamonds in the cave next door.

As we were walking into the room the sparkle of the diamonds we saw were so pretty that we decided to chip some off and then we left and we started on our quest again and went down the hallway and soon we were room where there was statues of all the gods and then I saw a god with a cat at his feet.

The problem was his feet were higher than my head and so I knew that I had to climb.

So I began to climb and when I got to his feet I noticed that there was almost no way down to his feet.

So I jumped, which was a big mistake because I had almost fallen off and hurt my ribs.

After a few minutes of laying there in pain I looked over and saw a lever beside me and I got up still holding my ribs and pulled the lever and in the middle of the floor a hole started to open up and then a box appeared to be lifting up from the bottom.

I jumped down and went over to the box and opened it and when I did the others went over to me and I looked inside the box and inside was a note that read: go past the dog that has no footprints and past the yelling walls through the moaning crystal caves and into the hallway of death and you shall find the sixth clue.

We started walking again and soon we were in another hallway but this one didn't make any noise or have anything to do with death so we continued walking until we came onto some crystal that were white as could be but didn't moan.

So we just kept on walking until we finally heard barking in the distance and then after a few minutes more of walking we saw a dog that was tied to a huge chain.

I walked up to it and saw that the paws made no mark and then I saw that the chains were not real which made the dog not real as well.

Then we started walking again and we started listening for the next part of the note {the yelling walls} and after a few minutes of walking we could hear yelling In the distance and we thought that it had to be the yelling walls in the distance.

We kept on going and then we came to a tunnel that the yelling seemed to be coming from and we started walking down this tunnel and soon we came to this wall and everything seemed to silence and we knew that we had to climb the wall and as we were about to climb the wall a wind came out of nowhere (literally since we are underground) and made the most horrid noise and I knew that we were on the yelling walls and why they were called that.

We continued up the yelling walls and when we made it to the top we were so glad to be off the walls that we actually danced for a few seconds and then we started walking again.

After a few moments have passed we began to hear a different noise...a moaning.

We came to a hallway that seemed to have many doors and soon we were hearing it a little louder at a time and then when we were right on it we could hear it loud and clear.

Then we turned a corner and we saw the most brilliant diamonds that you could ever lay your eyes on and they seemed to be vibrating like crazy.

Then danyelle picked off a piece of it and when she did the ground gave out from underneath her and she barely had time to grab the side of the hole that had been made when she plucked the diamond and then when finally got her back in the room I noticed the hole in the wall that had a eight sided edge.

I then took the crystal from danyelle and put it into the hole and a secret door appeared and we went through it and on the other side was a hallway that was blood red and at the end was a door that we went through.

When we did, we found a bedroom the size of a large master bedroom.

Then we started to have a look around and then I remembered that if we moved the bed then we would find a hole behind it but when we did there was nothing there except a bare wall.

Then I turned my head as danyelle was walking by and I saw a gold chest inside and I walked over to it and said in a joking manner "how did we miss this?"

I opened it and had to cover my eyes until the light dimmed as usual and then I picked up the tablet and read it: go past the roaring waterfall and through a veil and up a flight of stairs and down some pass the doors on the right and through the next one and you will have the seventh note to the seventh clue.

We started past the waterfall and stayed a good distance away so we wouldn't get plummeted from the force of the waterfall and then we started walking along the wall.

Then I noticed that there was a portion of the wall that looked different than the rest and so I went up to it but as soon as I got to it, the wall seemed to change back.

I went back to the others and asked them to follow me and then we went up to that wall and I reached out my hand and went to touch the wall but my hand seemed to pass right through it even though it seemed solid.

I saw that my hand went through and that when it did it seemed to turn a lighter shade and so I pushed my entire body through the wall and on the other side was a hallway.

I walked a bit of a distance from the wall so the others could get through and when they did they looked around and when they were done we started walking again.

After a few minutes of walking we came to a flight of stairs and we knew that we had to go up those stairs.

After a few minutes of walking up what felt like an elevator's worth of stairs we finally came out on level ground and was immediately followed by a staircase that went down and we also knew that we had to go on this one as well.

After we got on firm ground again we started down the hallway that we were in and after a while the hallway seemed to start sprouting doors.

We stopped at one door and was about to open it and then remembered that we had to go past the ones on the right and after a while the doors stopped and then there was only one door to the left of us.

When we saw that door to the left we went through it and saw that we were in another room that had a bed and everything.

When I saw that it had a bed I looked behind the bed and saw that there was nothing there and so we started looking around for a box or chest of any kind and after a few minutes found it.

The chest was in a corner covered by a few boxes that were empty and after I moved the boxes I saw the chest and I looked around to see that the others were beside me.

When I noticed that they weren't I motioned for them to come over to where I was and then when they was ready I opened the chest and inside was a scroll that read: go past the pond of souls and through the tunnel of love and open the door with the two and you shall have the seventh clue.

We started walking again and soon we were in an enormous room that had a pool the size of the base of olympus and we started looking around the room because there was no exit other than the one that we had just come through.

We looked for a good few hours and after those good few hours I sat down on a rock pillar and when I did I began to sink.

Then I got up and saw that it was nearly gone and then at that very moment we began to hear grinding.

Then we began to look around for doors but when I was searching for doors I saw that there was a lever right beside the river and so I went up to it and pulled it to find that it began to open a door at the far end of the room.

We went through that door and when we did it shut behind us and we started moving forward anyway.

We continued down that hallway and soon we started hearing singing and then I figured that the hallway was called the tunnel of love.

As we walked we began to hum the tune that was in the tunnel and then we came to a door that had two locks on it.

We started looking for the first key and after a few moments I saw a light coming from a corner of the room so I went over to it and I saw that it was a key that had a jewel in it.

So I picked it up and then I went up to the first key on the door and put it in.

When I put it in, the key began to turn and then the lock fell to the ground and then we started looking for the second key.

We started to get tired and sat down and when I did there was a rumbling and then a door opened to the side and we were about to go through when I remembered that we had one more key to go before we could move on.

We started searching for the second key and soon found it in a corner by where the entrance used to be and I put it into the last lock on the door.

When the door opened it revealed a small shelf with a few things on it and one of those things was a chest that was golden so we pulled it down and opened it.

When we did we had to shield our eyes until the blinding light went away then we looked inside the chest to see another golden tablet.

I picked it up and I read the tablet: travel back and go through that door through the mushrooms that give off spores past the crystals that are all so clear and past the singing that all may hear pass the lake that is ice see through clear and you may find the eighth clue my dear.

We started through the other door that was in the same room that the chest was and we went through that hallway and soon we came into a huge room that had some trees in the far end.

When we got closer we noticed that they were not trees at all, they were giant mushrooms and the spores that they were giving off were making us drowsy so we started past those.

We started towards where we thought that there would be an opening and soon saw that there wasn't any.

The only thing that was there was a crystal clear gem and so I walked up to it and then I had a thought come into my mind and I picked up a rock from a nearby hill and threw it at it but missed it the first time so I threw it again but this time I hit it dead on and it rang.

As it rang a door opened to the right of it and we went through and saw that it led to a cave that was full of clear crystals and then I noticed that there was a hole in front of them.

I pulled one of the crystals out of the ground and saw that one of these crystals would fit that hole so we started pulling them out and trying them on the hole.

With very few left we finally got the right one and it began to glow white and then a white outline appeared on the wall and we walked through it to find ourselves in a room where we could hear singing coming from the walls.

As we were going we came out into this room that also had clear crystals in it and we continued on until we came out into a large room.

There were three levers that were all around that room and from the look of things they all had to be pulled at the same time.

I walked up to one as danyelle and athero also grabbed one.

We pulled down all at once and a door opened and we went through to find ourselves in another large room and this one had a large icy lake in it.

We walked across the lake and saw that there was a chest under the ice and so I summoned a couple of lighting bolts and struck the ice, shattering it.

When the ice shattered we fell through and the chest was in front of us. I walked up to the chest and opened it and inside was a scroll that read: go through this door and past the vines that separate death and life and charge forward with full strife and then and only then can you open the locked door. Once through that door you shall see the chest that holds clue number eight.

As we were reading a door opened right in front of us going down so we started down that hole and pretty soon we were falling down a pipe and we landed in a heap.

When we got up we saw that we were in a whole different room and we started looking around to find that we were in some field and soon we found out that we would have to find the next part in this field so we started looking for the vines that separate life and death.

We looked around but couldn't see any vines, period and then athero started walking past us and then we started to see where he was going.

So we rushed to get back up to where he was at and then we saw the vines at the far end of the field.

When we saw the vines we started towards it then when we got to it we knew that we had to go past it and when we turned the corner we saw a door in the corner of the field so we started towards it and then we went through it and found ourselves running and out of breath.

We were about to run off the cliff but then we stopped just in time and turned the corner right through another door.

This door threw us into another field and on the far end was the door that had the keys and then I noticed that there were five giant keys that we had to find for the five giant locks.

We started looking for the first key and after a few hours I saw it by the door and I went over and tried to pick it up but I couldn't so I asked the others to help.

They came over and stopped what they were doing and started helping me put the key into the first lock.

When we finally got the first key into the hole, the key started to turn and the lock clicked open and we started to search for the second key.

After a few minutes we finally found it by the door that we had come through and we picked it up and put it into the second lock and it turned as well then we started searching for the third one.

We continued searching for the third one and soon we found that one as well and when we did we went to the third lock and together we put it into the lock and it turned the opposite direction.

We went looking for the fourth one and soon found it in a corner and I picked it up and it was considerably lighter than the others so I put it into the fourth lock myself.

Then we started looking for the last one and then I noticed that I was standing on it and I picked it up and went up to the last lock and put that key into it and it started turning counter clockwise like the last one and then the last lock clicked and they all dropped in almost unison and the door creaked open.

We walked forward and we found ourselves in a large room and in the corner was a small box that had a lid on it and we went up to the box and I pulled the lid off and peered inside.

Inside was a note that was on a thin piece of scroll and when I picked it up to read it, I dropped it and realized that it was freezing yet burning hot and I picked it up again and this time I could hold onto it and I read it.

What it said was: go through the blood red hallway and down the ghostly river and through the hollow wall pass the eagle in the sky and the and the rocks that ask why and you shall find the ninth clue.

As we were reading a door opened up in the wall nearest to us and we started to go to it and then we saw that it was closing and so we began to run but the faster we ran the faster it went down.

We slid under the door just in time for it to shut. When we were on the other side we saw that we were in a hallway and it didn't look too inviting so we just kept on walking.

Then I noticed something: the walls were a red color as if they were bleeding and then I knew that we were in the blood red hallway.

We continued walking until we finally came to the end of that hall and ran into yet another door and we went through that door, we found ourselves in another room and we started to explore and then I noticed a wall of boxes that was up against the corner and I went to check them out.

When we had all the boxes moved we saw that there was a river behind it and that isn't the weirdest part, there were spirits in the water.

We walked up to the water and then we saw the barrels and we each grabbed one and went to the river and stepped into the barrels and we started to float down the river.

Then I heard screaming and I knew that we were going down a waterfall with the spirits and when we landed we ended up on the shore and we quickly got on our feet so the spirits couldn't get us.

We looked around for a door but all we could see was rock trees and we needed to find a hollow door and then it clicked…trees are hollow so we needed to find a hollow tree formation.

We started looking around the formations and knocking on them and then finally on the second to last one we knocked on it and it sounded hollow and when we did we tried to knock again but my hand went through and it pulled my body with it and I soon found myself in another hallway.

Soon the others followed. The first one came through before I could even get up and then we were just waiting on danyelle.

As soon as she came through we headed out and soon found out that we were in an underground world and we started looking around and when we looked up we could see the shape of an eagle and we knew that it had to be the one from the scroll and we kept on walking.

After a while of walking we came to this cave and we saw that many of the rocks going up looked like question marks and then we walked across the room and soon we were in another room that could fit a whole dining room set in it.

In the corner was a gold chest and we went up to it and I opened it to see what was inside although I was pretty sure I already knew.

When I opened it we had to look away because the light was so bright. Once the light had dimmed I looked inside and we noticed that there was a tablet and a key that said: use me at your most dire time of need.

I picked up the tablet and the key and when I picked up the key I pocketed it and took the tablet and read it and it said: go past the fiery lake and through the ice caverns go through the lava corridor and after that you will have to unlock the door to the clue to the third piece.

THE TRIDENT OF POSEIDON ~ { 87 }

As we were reading a door opened in the far wall and we started towards it and that is when I noticed that it was slowly closing.

We hurried through the door and found ourselves in a hallway that seemed to open up into a room and when it did we saw that we were in the first part of the tablet and we started looking for a way out and that is when I saw the four buttons on the ground and I knew that there was only three of us.

So I started looking for a big enough boulder and when I thought I had found one I picked it up and put it onto the button and we got onto the others but no door opened.

So I threw the boulder aside and picked up another one and set it onto the button and we got onto the buttons again but this time the water in the pond began to drain down a hole in the bottom of the lake and I just knew that we had to follow.

So I motioned for the others to follow and I jumped through and landed in ice cold water and a few moments later I heard two splashes and then I surfaced and saw the others coming up for air.

Then I noticed that the water was ice cold so I started swimming towards the shore and when I got there I was warm all of a sudden.

I felt myself and found out that it was because I was dry to the bone again and then I picked myself up and started walking again and saw a red glow coming from the hallway up ahead and then I looked around and saw that we were in an ice cavern and I knew what came next.

We started walking and we walked through a cave that had some diamonds in it and then I became aware of the danger that we were in and I knew that we had to get through this quickly because we were in a volcanic tube that was still active.

We walked to the light and found out that it was the hallway that was shaped of lava and we began to hurry because we could see the light start to grow and then we found ourselves in front of a door.

We turned around and there was a wall of lava coming our way and then I noticed that the door that we had just come through could possibly hold it.

We pushed the doors closed and then when we did the doors vanished, replaced with a wall and the door appeared on the other side of the room and we went to open it.

When we did we found out that it was locked and then danyelle pointed out that there was a pattern on the door and then danyelle began to push the door and when she did I noticed that the pattern would light up.

Then after a few tries she got it open and when it did we saw that it wasn't the same thing that we had come through, it was a room and the room had a chest that needed a key.

I knew that I had to find this key and so I went to looking for the key but first I took a good look at the chest and then I had a pretty good idea of what the key would look like and after a few hours of looking I saw the key but it was way out of my grasp and then I looked around and tried to find a way to the key and then I saw the ledge.

I began to climb and after a few moments I was on the first ledge and I had to find a way to get to the second one without making the first one fall so I looked around and saw a vine nearby.

I grabbed the vine and swung across to the second the the third where the key hung and then I jumped down.

Once I had landed I went to the chest and put the key into it

And turned it and inside was the clue to where the third part was.

I looked inside and saw that there was a piece of scroll inside and I picked it up and read in my head.

It said: go through the crystal haze and past the golden water and you shall find the third piece when you have all you have.

As I was reading we heard a rumbling and I looked up and saw that there was a door opening and as I finished I began to walk towards it.

When I got to the other side I saw that the others had followed me then I looked around and saw that we were in another hallway.

When we looked down the hall we saw that the other end looked like it was twisting and swerving to the left and right.

We walked up to it and soon we could barely keep our balance. Before long we were almost on our faces and then I noticed that we were almost to the other end of the hall.

I started crawling for the other side and as soon as I did the others noticed and followed suit. When we finally got to the other side we started to feel more normal again.

Once we felt normal again we started through the end of the hall and went into the next room.

What we found was an amazing sight, there was a large pool of water that was bright yellow.

Almost as if it was liquid gold so I decided that I would test it and I picked up a stone and dipped it partly into the water and the part that was dipped had turned a goldish color.

We started looking around and soon we had found a hole in the wall so I stuck my hand in.

All I could think about was all those movies about getting your hands chopped off in a hole in the wall.

Then I felt something in the hole and I gripped it and pulled. Immediately a hidden hallway opened.

We went through although quite aware and then athero accidently touched the wall and yelped in pain.

I looked at him and then at the wall and saw that the wall was kind of a red color and I knew that there had to be lava behind it.

We kept on walking without touching the walls and then we came to the end which landed us at a brick wall.

All of us knew what we had to do and we touched it at the same time and we didn't get sucked in this time we got warped.

When we came to we saw that we were in another room but this one was quite smaller and higher than the others.

In the middle of the room was a statue of Poseidon and in his hand was the third piece.

I put it with the others and as I watched the piece melted back into its place on the trident.

Then one of the tablets that I had kept on me started to glow in my bag and athero pointed it out. I looked at him and then my bag and pulled it out.

When I did the tablet stopped glowing and I saw that it was blank now and then I noticed that there were lines that were being etched into it as we looked at it.

When the lines stopped etching, I saw that it was the name Nemrut Dagi and I said to the others" well I think we know where we have to go next".

I looked at the others then nodded and we rolled our magic marbles and thought of Nemrut Dagi and a portal opened for us to go through.

When we got to the other side we saw that we had jumped into some ruins which wasn't abnormal for us and we started looking around in the hot sun.

{ five }

Mt.Nemrut

As I said we started looking around in the hot...no blistering sun and soon saw that we were in another easter island ruin.

We started to look around and after a few moments I had an Idea that the glyph could be on one of the heads.

So I started looking at the heads and after a few moments of looking the others started looking at me wondering what I was doing.

I told them to start looking at the sides of the heads for the glyph. After a few moments we had searched almost every head in the vicinity and as I was walking up to the last to I went to the one on the right, the one on the left caught my eye.

I turned towards the one to the left and went up to it to find engravings on it and as I was running my fingers over it the lines began to light up.

I called the others over to me and as they were coming over I realized that I still had my hand on the statue's head and my hand started to heat up and before I knew it I was laying on my back.

I laid on my back for a few minutes and then I got up and looked up to where I fell from and it seemed like a really far distance.

Then I saw a body falling down and when It came to a soft halt I noticed that it was athero and then athero yelled really loud to danyelle.

We saw danyelle floating down the hole gracefully until she made it to the ground and we started to have a look around.

Soon we saw that we were in a cave that was similar to the last one that we were in and then we started to see golden writing appear on the wall and after a few moments we saw that it was the first note.

We started to read the words and the words read: go down the hall of death and the red hall of lava through the waterfall and into the crystal room then down the hall to the hidden room and you shall find the first clue of four to the fourth trident piece.

As we were reading, we saw that there was a dark door to the left of us and we started towards it. As we were going down the hallway the darker it got and this time there was no torch to light the way.

When I saw that it was dark, I created a small lighting surge on my hand and it gave a little light to the hallway and when it did we saw that the hall was made with skulls in it.

We began to walk as fast as we could and soon we could see the light at the end of the tunnel.

When we could we started towards it and soon we were at the end and we came into a room that was red and it had a lava river with giant flat rocks coming down it so we went across the river and then we started down the hall that was a lot like the room.

I put my hand on the wall which was a mistake because the second I did I yelped because the wall had burnt my hand.

We started down the hallway in silence without touching the walls at any time and almost as soon as we had started down the hall we were almost to the end and we saw a little light glistening at the end of the hallway, and I knew that the waterfall was almost upon us.

Before we knew it we were being soaked and we knew that we were under the waterfall and we started forward a little at a time.

While we were walking forward, I noticed that I seemed to be sinking and then I noticed that I was in sand...not just any sand quicksand.

I grabbed onto the rock wall and started pulling myself free and once I was free, I looked around for an easier way across and soon found it going off to the side.

I started walking and soon I was in the next room. Then I noticed that there were not any crystals in this room, so I went into the hallway that was to the left.

As we walked down this hallway, we started to see crystals in the hall, and I knew that we were going the right way and then the hallway curved to the left.

We started down this part of the hall and after a while we came up to a rock wall and I knew that if I touched it I would get sucked through but I did it anyway.

I reached out my hand and it pulled me through with so much force that I almost had a whiplash.

When I got up after the dizziness had gone away I had a look around and saw that I had found the secret room although it wasn't much of a secret room.

I waited for the others to go through and after a few minutes they came flying into me and I had to pick myself up off the floor a second time.

Once we were all in the hidden room we started looking for the chest that would hold the first tablet that would tell us where to go next but found the exit first.

We started searching the walls first but there wasn't anything there so we started combing the room.

We checked the boxes first and then athero moved a barrel to get to a box and uncovered a button.

As soon as the button was undone a lever came out of thin air on the other side and so I went up to it and pulled it and that opened a trapdoor that lifted.

When it was done we saw that it had the chest in it and we walked up to it and saw that it was an old chest by the looks of it and we opened it and inside was the first tablet.

We looked at it and then words started to show on it and when it was done, I read it and it read: go down the liquid hallway and through the crystal chamber and past the monster illusions and you will find the second note to the second tablet.

When we were done reading, I noticed that there was a hallway leading to the left and I started down that hallway.

That hallway wasn't very long and then I came into another room that had a pond in the center and I looked into it and saw that it had a swirl in the center of it and I knew that we had to go swimming in order to get to it.

I got in and dove down and I turned around in mid-swim and saw the others right behind me and then suddenly, I was brought to the ground and I saw that I was in a watery hallway.

We started down the hallway and then we noticed that there was a wall of water at the end that I was at and I expected that it would be that way on the other side and we started walking as soon as everyone was there.

As soon as we were all here we went down that hallway and soon we were on the other side and soon we were in the water again.

When we got done swimming and we were in dry land again we saw that there were crystals all over the room and we knew that we were in the right place.

We went towards the hall leading off to the next room and then I saw a shadow but I knew that it had to be an illusion like in the note.

Then I got a good look at it and I could see that it was an illusion and we started walking down that hall into the next room and soon we were in another room that almost looked like a bedroom that was a burial tomb.

We started looking around and soon we had found a chest that was as old as the room and I went up to it and went to open it.

As I opened it dust poured into the air and we held our breath for as long as we could. When It finally cleared I looked in the chest to find a piece of parchment.

I picked up the piece of parchment and turned it over and saw that it was the second note to the second clue out of four.

I looked it over and then I started to read and it read something like this: go through the under veil and around the waterfall of liquid gold past the dark hallway and finally undo three locks on a door and you will find the next clue.

We started walking and we turned a corner and soon we were face to face with a wall so we started searching for a switch and then danyelle pointed to a hole in the wall and I saw that it was just big enough to put my hand in.

I put my hand in the hole and began to feel around and then I felt something round, and I pulled on it and the wall shifted aside.

I began to hear cracking in the hole and I pulled my hand out in time to hear a thud come from the hole where my hand would have been.

Then I went through the hole where the wall was and into the room beyond and when I did the door closed behind me and we were trapped in the room that we were in.

We started to have a look around and soon I found a door that was see through and red. I walked up to it and ended up walking right through it and I found myself in the underworld.

I instantly searched for the other door because the one that I had gone through closed as soon as the others went through it as well.

Soon we were pushed through a hole and ended up in another room in the same tunnel that we were in before.

Then up ahead we could hear crashing and we knew what was coming up but we also knew that we had to pass it.

We walked up to the yellow waterfall and I threw a piece of long rock that I found on the ground and the rock melted into molten rock.

Then I saw a path leading around the melted gold and we started down that path and into the room beyond.

As we were walking I noticed a hallway that was black at night and when I got used to the dark I noticed that there were shadows.

We kept on walking and after a few minutes we came to a door that had three locks on it that it was talking about.

I noticed that there was a certain pattern on each lock and I knew that there would be the same pattern on the key as well.

So we started looking around for the first key and after a few moments we found the third one so I got the key from danyelle and put it into the third lock and turned and to my amazement the lock disappeared.

Then we started looking for the first one and once again we didn't find the one that we were looking for because we had found the second key instead of the first one.

I walked over to the second lock and turned that one and it also disappeared and then we started looking for the only key left.

We had only started looking for that one when I saw something shining on the ground and I walked over to it and saw why we couldn't find the first key.

It was partly buried and danyelle must have kicked it or something because I could see it now.

I picked it up and went back to the locks and when I turned instead of disappearing the doors disappeared and we walked through.

When we were in the doors came back and we were locked in and I saw a hallway leading off to the left and right and there was a chest in the center of the room.

We walked up to the chest and I opened it and inside was the second golden tablet and as usual there was a golden light that we had to wait out.

When the light was gone I looked at the tablet and I knew that it was the second clue out of four and I picked it up and looked over it.

As I was looking it over words started to appear and we read together: go down the hall and past the rubies, the sapphires, and then the emeralds and you will find the third note.

As I was reading a door slid open going down. We looked at each other and I said" do we really have a choice?"

We went down the stairs and into a damp hallway and I knew that we had to be under some water for it to be this damp.

We continued walking and then we came into a room that had a large ruby cluster in the center of the room.

We knew that we had to just keep walking and soon we had found the sapphires as well and we were well on our way to finding the emeralds.

After a few moments of walking we began to wonder if we were going the right way and then athero pointed out the green flickers.

We walked that way and soon we were in a room that had a tremendous amount of emeralds in it and we walked out the only other hallway that was there.

As we were walking down that hall we saw tons of rooms and then at the end of the hall it opened up into a larger room than the others.

This room was covered in broken vases and then I spotted the chest in the corner.

I went up to it and opened it and when I did I expected something abnormal but all that was in the chest was a note that I knew was the third note to the third clue.

Then I picked it up and read it and it read: go past the golden arch and through the veil to the other side past the diamonds and past the first field and into the next one and you shall find the third clue in the forest.

When we got done reading, we heard a rumbling and we looked up and saw that a was opening in front of us.

We started forward and on the other side of the door was the longest hallway that I had ever seen.

We started walking and after a while we came into a room that was filled with gold but there weren't any arches.

So we kept on going and we must have made a wrong turn or something because the next room we came to was filled with diamonds.

We walked right past that room and we came back to the same room and then I saw a hallway that was blending in.

I pointed it out to danyelle and we went into it and we had to make sure that we didn't trip because the hall we were in was made out of diamonds.

I looked back and saw athero stumble and almost crash into some pointy crystals but I caught him just in time and almost slipped myself.

Then a few minutes into tripping and stumbling we made it to the other side and saw that we were in another gold room and in the center was the golden arch.

We walked up to it and then went through and as I did I felt a wave of energy come over me and we saw a hallway going off to the right.

We walked down that hallway for a while and then the hallway took a turn to the left and when we did, we saw a couple doors leading off.

We kept on walking and soon we were in a room that was empty except for two columns and between the two columns was a mist.

We walked up to it and I knew that we had to go through that and it would transport us to where we needed to go.

So one by one we walked up to it and went through until it was my turn and when I went into the veil I was suddenly in a transport tunnel.

When it spit me out, I was in another room and I could see a field that was the first one that we had to pass by.

So we started walking and soon the path that we were walking on came out into a field and we saw that there were stone trees on the far end.

We started going towards the rock forest and between the trees we saw the chest that held the third clue.

We tried to walk through but the trees made some sort of barrier then I saw that the bottom had large holes in it so we started through the holes in the bottom.

Then about an hour later, we got to the chest and was amazed to find that we could stand up.

I walked up to the chest and opened it and when I did the light almost blinded me (that is how bright it was).

I stepped back until the light lessened up and then I picked up the tablet and read: go through the doors ahead and past the silver archway and then a gold one then up one staircase and down the second and you shall find the fourth note in the fourth door to the right.

When we were reading, we saw the door flicker, and i seen athero walk right through it, so we followed.

Once we were on the other side we saw that we were in a room that had silver all over but there was no archway that we could see.

We started to have a look around because we didn't see any doors and then I saw it...the silver arch and below it was a flickering wall.

I motioned for the others to follow me and I went through the flickering wall and saw that we were in another room.

Then we saw that this room was filled with diamonds, but the clue didn't say anything about a diamond room.

But in the corner, we saw that there was a golden arch there but there wasn't any door there flickering or otherwise.

So we started to have a look around and soon I found a lever that I could not pull alone so I called on athero to help and together we got the lever down.

When we pulled the lever, the floor opened up, and three buttons appeared, and I started to have a look around to find something heavy to put on them.

Then I saw the picture on the wall, and it showed three beings standing on the buttons and the door opened.

So we all got on one button each and then we heard click...click...click and the door flickered.

We started walking towards it and when we got there we walked right through and when we got to the other side we saw that we were in a room that had a staircase going up and so we walked up the stairs.

After we got to the top we found another set of stairs going back down so we took the stairs down and found that this one didn't go down as far as the last one.

When we got to the bottom of the stairs we saw that we were in a hallway and there were doors to the left and right.

We started counting the doors to the left because we knew that the note would be in the fourth door.

When we got to four, we went through that door and found ourselves inside a bedroom and in the corner was a chest.

We walked up to the chest and I opened it and inside was the fourth note and I picked it up and read: past the vibrating stones and past the lava river and through the five lock door and you shall find the fourth clue.

We saw a door open in front of the chest and we knew that it was the way that we had to go through.

We went through that door and found ourselves in a hallway that was filled with stones and as we got close to them they started to vibrate at such a high frequency that we had to cover our ears.

We finally made our way through that hallway and found ourselves in another room that had more of the exact same rocks but these were bigger.

These rocks were so big that they were making the wall vibrate and we looked for another way out and I saw a lever that could open a passage out of the vibrating room.

So we walked up to the lever and I looked it over but it looked like all we had to do was pull it so I grabbed it and pulled and it went all the way down. The wall didn't open but the stones stopped vibrating.

Then athero said" so that is what it does". When he said that we all looked at him and then we started to look around for a way out.

As we were looking I started to feel the wall and then I started to get a weird feeling as if I had been here before and then I knew why.

There was the same painting that we had seen before on the wall in front of me and then I noticed the two holes in the wall and I knew that I had to put my hands in and pull the levers inside.

I put my hands in and could feel the levers and then I grabbed them and pulled and then a door opened and I pulled my hands out in time to not get them cut off.

We went through the door and found ourselves in front of a river of lava and then I noticed the five levers.

Then I saw that three of the levers already had keys in them but they were not turned so we started looking for key number three and five.

We found key number five first...that one was the easier one , it was on top of a box and I noticed it right away.

I put it into the keyhole and then we started to search for the third one and after a few minutes we had found the last one and we put the last one.

we turned all of them and after we turned them, we started towards the edge of the lava river.

As we neared the edge we saw that the river of lava was quickly being blocked by a blockade and we went to move but as we were nearing the other side the river started to overflow.

So we began to run as fast as we could and barely made it and then we headed for the door and when we got there we noticed that there were five keys for that as well.

We started searching for the keys then I noticed that danyelle was just standing there and I asked her if she was going to help and she just shook her head no.

I looked at her confused and then she went up to the door and put her hand into her pocket and pulled out the keys from the levers and began to put them into the locks and then she turned them and to my amazement they opened the door.

I turned to her and asked " how did you know that those keys would work for the door?" she shrugged and said "just a hunch".

We walked past the door and soon we were in a small room that was way undersized for the doors that we had to go through to get to the room that we were in.

We started to have a look around and soon I spotted the chest that had the final tablet in it for this place.

I walked up to the chest and opened it and had to step back to let the light die down. Once the light had died down I picked up the tablet and saw that lettering was starting to appear on it.

Once the words stopped I started reading them with the others beside me. It read something like: go past the howling halls and through the glacial water to the other side and you shall find the last note for this place.

As we were reading we began to hear howling in the near distance and so we started walking towards it.

After a few minutes of walking we could almost hear the howling clearly now and we knew that we had to be close by.

We turned a corner and we knew that we were right in front of it and we walked into the tunnel and all around us we could hear howling and we knew that we were in the howling halls.

Once we were through that hallway we saw that we had come out into a room that had a large pool in it and I knew that it had to be freezing.

The other two didn't just feel the water they jumped in and started to swim so I did the same thing and hoped for the best.

I saw the other side almost as soon as I jumped in because it was clear as day in the water and we kept on swimming to the other side where we reached the other side and broke the surface of the water.

We got out of the water and I saw a hallway to the right that shimmered with light and I headed for that and then I noticed that my clothes were dry.

I continued towards the end of the hall and found out that it led to a room that had the last chest in it for this place.

I went up to it and saw that it was lidless and I looked at it and saw that the note was still there but it was on a silver tablet that read: go past this gate and through this portal to the room where the fourth part of the trident of Poseidon is and you shall find your destination.

We looked forward but didn't see any kind of gate but that didn't mean that there wasn't one there.

So I walked forward and the wall started to flitter and then it shifted moving blocks to the side and pushed them up or down and started to open to reveal a hallway and as it was finishing I began to see that it was the gateway that it was talking about.

When it was done I looked over the gateway and saw that the top lipped over the door itself was a grayish color that we would have to pass through and on it the door said: pass through to find the end.

We walked forward and went through the muddy surface that made us have to hold our breath until we were through and then we saw that we were in another room that was on the other side and I knew that the portal had to be in here somewhere.

I waited for the others to get through the goop and when they finally got through we started looking around the room for some kind of portal and we were about to quit all together.

Then I noticed that there was a purple necklace in the corner that had a vortex on the big bead and I thought that I had found it so I focused on it and saw that it was a useless trinket.

Then I saw the wall in the far edge of the room move and I knew that it had to be the portal so I motioned for the others to follow me and I went through the wall and on the other side we saw a statue of Poseidon.

Then I saw the fourth piece of the trident on the statue and I reached up and with help from athero I got the second point of the trident and then I said "just one more to go now" as I was looking at it.

We took another look at the map and It said: Leonidas statue, Thermopylae.

Then Atheros' eyes lit up and said "yeah I know that place my mom took me there once and we pulled out our portal marbles and focused on Thermopylae and we were instantly transported there.

When we got there we were hit with a blast of sunshine and we loved to be back in the fresh air.

{ six }

Thermopylae

When we got out of the portal that our marble made we found that we were greeted by the sun and it felt good to breathe in fresh air again.

Then we started looking for the statue of Leonidas and almost as soon as we started looking for it we saw it in the distance.

We walked up to it and started to look over it and then I saw the glyph and when I touched it I got sucked in and started to fall and when I landed it was as if I fell a short distance.

Then I looked above me and saw that I did only fall a short distance and then I saw the others falling and I stood up and watched them land.

When they were getting up I started to take a look around and I saw that we were in the same type of starter cave that we were in with the last place.

Then I began to see letters on the wall and they said: go down this hall and to the left and into the field of the bass clef past the trees and you shall find the first note.

We started looking around for a hallway and after a few moments we started to see a hallway in the darkness as our eyes adjusted.

We walked towards that hallway and then we saw that there was a dark hallway there and we started down it.

When we were about half way down the hall it began to curve to the left and then we started walking again.

Then out of nowhere we passed through a wall and we were in a field and we had to cover our ears because the bass was so low.

It was then that we knew that we were in the bass field and we started looking for the trees but they were nowhere to be found and then I saw an open door and we walked through that instead.

When we were through the doors the first thing we saw were the trees that it had mentioned in the words on the wall and so we went up to the trees because they were not very far away and started looking for the first note.

When we finally got to the trees we went through them and finally saw the first chest that would hold the first note and I walked up to it.

I saw that this one was made of silver and I opened it to find the first note inside.

I picked up the note and read it to the others and this is what it said: go through the hallway of screams and the lava river with five keys and through the ice and fire arch and you shall find the first clue.

When we got done reading we stood still for a moment but couldn't hear anything but the soft but rapid sound of our breathing.

We started walking again and soon we saw a hallway up ahead and as we got closer we started to hear the most blood hurling scream.

Then we knew that it was the hallway of screams and we just held our ears and passed through the hallway and went as far away from it as possible.

Then when the tunnel of screams stopped then we saw that we were in another room but the room and the edge of a lava river was close by.

We took a look around and saw that there were five levers on the side of the river and they all needed keys.

Then I noticed that the levers were numbered in roman numerals and I knew that the keys would have the same number on them.

We started looking for the keys and soon we found key number three and I got it from athero.

Then I put it into the third lever and turned it. Then we started looking for the other keys and almost right after I had started looking again athero had found another one and gave it to me.

I walked up to the fifth lever because it was the fifth key and I turned it. Then I rejoined the others in looking for the keys.

Then not long after I saw the number two just barely poking out of the sand and I picked it up and put it into the second lever.

Then I turned it and then started looking for the key number one and key number four and soon I saw a keyring on the wall and I picked it and looked it over.

When I did I found key number one but not key number four and I put key number one in the lever and turned it and then I started looking for key number four.

When I was about to just give up I saw it like a star from my father. I cut it down with a cut of a bolt and put it into the fourth lever and turned it.

When I did, a red line appeared between the levers and then a door opened up along with a couple boulders on the lava.

We hopped across the boulders and walked up to the door and walked through the door right into the next room and when we arrived in the next room we could feel warmth and cold at the same time.

So we looked up and saw that we were passing under the icefire arch and I knew that the chest was near so we started looking around.

We finally found it in a corner of the room that we were in. I opened it and we stepped back because of the brilliance of the light that came out of the chest.

Once the light cleared I picked up the tablet that was inside and saw that words were starting to appear on the tablet and as we watched the clue wrote itself.

When it was done I read it to the others and it read: find the levers and keys and you shall cross the lava, once you do you will have to find the door and inside you will find the second note.

When I was done reading a door opened and we went through a hallway so we started down the hallway and after a few minutes we came into a room with a river of lava dividing it.

We knew that this was the lava that we had to cross so we started looking and the first thing that I noticed and pointed out to the others was the two holes in the ground.

I knew that the holes held levers but we had to find them first…even if they were not whole.

We started looking around for the levers or parts of the levers and then danyelle found the first piece and it was a pretty long piece too.

I saw that it was the middle of one of the levers so I held onto it and we started looking again. Then after about an hour of looking athero finally found another piece.

When he did he gave it to me and I put it with the other piece and when I put it in with the other one they merged and we saw that we only had one more piece for the first lever.

We got back to looking and soon danyelle had found another piece but it was another long piece.

Then she came up to me with the piece in hand and gave it to me so I put it into the backpack that I was carrying with the other one.

We went back to looking and after a minute of looking, athero came up to me and gave me a small piece and I knew that it had to be the last piece to the first lever.

I put it up to the first lever parts and the lever became whole. When it did I took it out of my bag and put it into the first hole and then went to look for the second piece of the second lever.

Almost as soon as I had started looking I found not the second but the third piece of the second lever and I held that piece in my hand and kept on looking.

After a few minutes of finding nothing I sat down against the wall and when I did I saw glittering.

As I turned to look I saw that it was the final piece and I went over to pick it up and then I connected it to the others and put it into the final hole.

Then athero and I, since you had to have feet in order to twist them, turned them and a pathway came up to the surface of the lava.

When it did we heard a clicking and we figured out real quick that it was on a timer.

Once we were on the other side we looked back to see the path sinking below the surface again.

When we saw that the pathway was gone we saw that there was a door ahead and we knew that we had to find the two keys that would go to the locks on the door.

When we got closer I saw that the locks had a weird pattern on them and a roman numeral one and two.

Then we started looking for the first key and soon we found the key that we weren't looking for.

When danyelle found it she gave it to me and I put it into the lock with the roman numeral two. Then we started looking for the key that we were originally looking for.

Then athero walked over to the corner and picked up something and then walked over to me and handed me the key that I guessed he had picked up.

I put the key into the other lock and when I did the keys turned and the door opened to reveal a room beyond.

We started looking around the room and soon saw a gold box against the far wall and I walked up to it and opened it.

Inside was a note that was laden in gold and shimmered in the light and read: go past the crystals, through the tunnel of light, up a flight or two and down one, and you shall find the third clue.

As we were reading a small door opened up and we got on our hands and knees and started down that tunnel for a few minutes and then it came out into a huge room but this room didn't have any crystals in it.

So we looked around and I saw a tunnel in the dark and I went into it and then Hollard for the others to follow so they didn't get lost.

Once they were by my side we walked down that hallway together and came into a room that was shining with amethyst and I knew that we were getting closer so we kept going.

We walked through a door to the left and found ourselves in a room with tons of quartz on the walls then we saw that there was just one door in the room that we were in and so we went through it.

When we went through that door we found ourselves in a room that was filled with rubies and there was a hallway leading off to the left so we took it.

When we went into it we saw that the hallway sparkled and had its own way of lighting up.

We came out into a room that was filled with sapphires and then we went through a door to the right.

When we did we came into a room that had a ton of diamonds in it and we knew that we couldn't take any of them so we went around looking for a way to the next room and soon found it behind the biggest crystal of all.

We went through that hallway and came into a room that had a staircase going up and I immediately started to go up and the others were hesitant to follow.

When they finally did I started to hear why there was a snoring growl that was coming from the top of the stairs.

We continued up the stairs but quietly and when we got to the top we saw that all the doors were closed and there was one door open and we knew that we had to go through that one.

We went through that door and found ourselves face to face with a giant but it was all chained up and asleep and we walked past it trying not to make any noise.

We walked to the stairs and started down them and we didn't release our tension until we were at the bottom of the stairs where we were safe.

Once we were away from the giant we continued walking down the stairs and came into a bedroom and then we started to look around and then I spotted the chest under the bed.

I went up to it and pulled the chest out and saw that it was made out of solid gold.

I opened the chest and Inside was the eighth clue and once I picked it up words started to appear and they said: go through the old tunnel that is rarely used, past the fires that were abused over the bridge and through the trees and you shall find the fourth note.

We started looking around and after a few minutes we finally found the door that would eventually lead to the old tunnel that is rarely used.

We went through that door and found ourselves in a tunnel that was filled with cobwebs and we continued walking and took the first door that we could and soon found that we had made a mistake that could have been fatal if we had closed the door.

When we looked around we saw that there was an ogre in the middle of the room and he was free but he hadn't noticed any of us yet.

So we quietly turned around and went back through the door and into the hall and soon we were at the end and we went through the opening at the end of the hallway.

When we did we came into a room that was filled with copper and they were glowing like they were on fire and we saw that the fire that was abused was the copper.

I started to look around and then I noticed the opening in the side of the wall that led off to the side and we went through that opening and came out in a room that had a big door in the center of one wall.

I noticed that there were two wooden bars across the door. I knew that no matter what we did we wouldn't be able to get that door open.

We just weren't tall enough to reach the second bar so I leaned up against it and to my surprise I fell through (looks like we didn't need to lift the bars after all.

When I got up I noticed that I was in a field and I looked around and I saw the trees in the distance and the bridge up ahead.

I motioned for the others to follow me out into the field and then we started to walk up to the bridge and as we were walking across it there was a rumbling and the bridge started to shake.

We ran to the other side and we barely made it there when the bridge broke into pieces and we started to run away.

Then we noticed that the trees were the other direction and we doubled back to the spot that we were at and then headed for the trees.

When we got to the trees I could see the gold box that would hold the fourth note in this place but there wasn't any place to get in.

Then I spotted the small hole near the wall and I got back down on my hands and knees and crawled through and found myself in a forest…an actual forest.

I walked up to the gold box and waited for the others to find their way into the forest and then I opened the box and inside was a parchment that had the fourth note on it and it shimmered like the other one did.

Then I picked it up and saw that it read: through this hallway and past the green through the double doors and past the sheen past the clock and the fifth clue is behind the lock.

When I read" lock" a door started to appear in the solid rock wall and once the hole was complete then I pushed it in and it fell backwards into the hallway.

When the wall door fell we went into the hallway and started to have a look around and soon we realized that we were in the hallway that was in the note.

We looked forward but couldn't see anything except darkness so I grabbed a torch and lit it so we would have light and then we started walking down the hall until we started to see doors on either side.

We continued walking until we were almost at the end of the tunnel and we could see a dim light at the end of it.

When we got to the end we saw that we had come out in a room that was filled with rubies and sapphires but no emeralds.

Then it began to make sense...the green must mean emeralds.

So we started walking through the door on the opposite wall and soon we were in another room and this one had green stones in it but they were not emeralds, they were peridots.

We started into the next room and soon we were walking in another hallway and when we reached the end of the hallway we saw that it ended in two doors and I knew that it was the double doors from the note.

We pushed open those doors and as soon as we did we saw that there was a silver pond in the center of the room and I knew that was the sheen that it was talking about.

We started walking again and then I noticed the homemade clock that was above a door so we went through that door and ended up in front of a locked door.

I'm guessing that we had to find the key and we started looking around the room. I started moving boxes and then danyelle knocked over a barrel and inside was the key to the lock.

We opened the door and saw that the door leads to a room that was filled to the brim with gold and copper and then I saw the chest in the corner of the room.

I walked up to it and went to open it and when I did the chest emitted such a bright light that I had to step back and wait for the light to clear.

When it did I walked up to the chest and saw the last tablet and when I picked it up words began to appear on it and I waited for the words to stop so I could read it.

When it finally stopped spelling I began to read: go past the crates and barrels and don't forget to look there will be a surprise in one go to the next room and move the gold that weighs a ton and you shall have access to the fifth note.

As we were reading a door began to open behind the chest and then we saw that there was a hallway behind it.

We stepped over the chest and started walking down that hallway and that is when we started to see the doors that were on the left side of the hall.

After a few more minutes of walking we finally started to see the crates and barrels and one by one we tipped them over to see what was inside.

We didn't find anything in any of the barrels until we knocked the last one over and a key came out danyelle grabbed it and then we started walking again.

We continued walking for a few minutes and then we came to a door and I tried to push it open and then I noticed that there was a lock on it and when I saw that I knew where the key went.

We opened the door and when I went through I saw that there was gold everywhere and I began to wonder how I would ever find the right gold pieces...or where to put them.

We started looking around and then I spotted the gold bars and then I knew what I had to do but I still didn't know where to put it.

I started to study the walls to see if they would give me any clue as to where to go.

I started to push on the walls and then apparently I had pushed a button or something because a part of the wall had slowly slid open to reveal two large buttons on the ground of the room.

I moved the bars of gold from near the chest to the complete other side of the room and after a few minutes of doing that back and forth I got tired and had to sit down.

When I was back up to full strength we continued until all the gold blocks were on the buttons and the wall started to go down so fast we barely got out.

When the door shut then another one started to open and we got ready to face anything and when we saw the box we knew what was in it...the fifth clue.

We walked up to the box and I opened it and read to the others: go to the field and by the trees into the hall and look for the bees and you shall find the sixth note.

When we were down reading a door started to open at the other end of the room and we started to walk towards it and by that time it was almost fully open and when we started to walk towards it the door began to close.

It was about halfway when I made it through and three quarters of the way down when the others made it.

When the door shut behind us we were surprised that we could still see in front of us.

We began to walk and before we knew it we were walking in a field and then I saw the trees that it was talking about.

So I began to walk towards them and saw that there was a similar hole beside them so I crawled through it to find myself in a hallway that had a line of bees going down the hall.

I followed the line and soon I found the bees base and beside it was the sixth box like it said and then I called for the others and noticed them beside me.

Then I opened the box and saw the note inside and picked it up and read it to the other two and it said: go through the fog and into the bog and you in front of an arrow you shall find a hole dive in and you shall find the trident.

When we were done reading a slimy hole opened in the ground and all of us jumped in and landed in a foggy swamp.

We started walking and then I spotted the arrow in the distance but we weren't coming any closer fast.

After about an hour of walking in a swamp we finally came to the arrow that was pointing down and I could barely see the hole and I jumped in and started to dive.

When I dove it didn't take me long to hit the other side and then I broke the surface. Then I got out of the water and there on the podium was the last piece to the trident of Poseidon, so I picked it up and pulled the rest of it out.

Then I put the last piece in place and then I could feel the might of the weapon and I made sure that the others were with me and then we all shouted mt.olympus as we rolled our marbles and we went through the portal that would lead us to mt. Olympus.

{ seven }

Home

When we came out of the portal we were near the gods temple and we walked up the stairs to the throne room.

When we got there we saw that Zeus, Poseidon, and the others were on their thrones.

I pulled out the trident and gave it back to Poseidon and he thanked me and then Zeus got another whisper in his ear and then Zeus announced to us that was brave.

With that we rolled our portal marbles into the wall and called out "camp demi-god."

When we got back, it was dark and we saw Chiron waiting for us and we came up to him and he raised his eyebrows and said " The whole camp heard what happened and you have had a long week. We are all in your debt.

Donald Carter lives in the bustling small city of cape Girardeau where he enjoys walking by the Mississippi river and reading he also loves going to the library and the book rack.

www.ingramcontent.com/pod-product-compliance
Lightning Source LLC
LaVergne TN
LVHW012053070526
838201LV00083B/4487